Praise for "An Imperfect Oath"

An engaging and page-turning story of two police officers, one on each side of the law, fighting against each other for the ultimate win.

Long and Short Review

The book is well written with enough suspense and tension to satisfy the most avid mystery lover. Grab a copy of this book but you may want to read it with the lights on.

Open Book Society

Praise for "Hunter/Hunted"

Hunter/Hunted is a chilling new novel that brings back Detective Carol Ward. Her new adversary is Skylar Topping, a young woman whose love for her family drives her to break the law. The action is fast paced and the characters are an eclectic mix that keeps the reader engaged.

Spice Girl – Amazon

The Secrets They Kept

Stewart Goodwin

Thank you to;
Becky, David, Janice, Kristen & Rhonda.
Without you this book would not have been possible.

The Secrets
They Kept

Stewart Goodwin

The Secrets They Kept©2019 by Stewart Goodwin. All rights reserved. No part of this book may be used or reproduced in any manner whatsoever, including Internet usage, without written permission from Stewart Goodwin, except in the case of brief quotations embodied in critical articles and reviews.

First Edition
First Printing, 2019

Book design and format by Stewart Goodwin
Cover design by Stewart Goodwin
Front cover photo ©Jada Callender
Back cover photo ©Stewart Goodwin

This book is a work of fiction. Names, characters, businesses, places, events and incidents are either the products of the author's imagination or used in a fictitious manner. Any resemblance to actual persons, living or dead, or actual events is purely coincidental. All characters are products of the author's imagination. Their actions took on a life of their own of which the author has no control. You know how kids are when left unsupervised by their parents.

Library of Congress Cataloging-in-Publication Data (pending)

ISBN 9798784812681

Published by Stewart Goodwin

"Three may keep a secret, if two of them are dead."
Benjamin Franklin

~1~

Sitting on the knoll just one hundred yards from the Cow Pasture River, the cabin had not seen human habitation in more years than one could count. With windows broken and doors askew, nature and critters had claimed it as a sanctuary from the elements. Thieves had entered and removed all of the piping leaving the plumbing inoperable. The sinks and tub had been claimed by someone as well. The wood siding had not received a coat of paint in too many years causing the wood to become thirsty for moisture of any kind. As the thirsty wood absorbed the moisture from the air, mold grew on the inside of the house. Large black patches had formed on the faded flowered wallpaper in the bedrooms and the paneling in the living room had a gray tinge announcing the growth of the mold behind. Being in such disrepair it seemed the only solution was demolition.

Trees had begun to reclaim the land that was once lush fields of green grass, golden wheat or vegetable gardens. Fields that had once produced enough fruit and vegetables to not only feed the family of seven who once filled the home with joy and laughter but also the surrounding community. Filling the back of the 1950's station wagon, the father and older children would drive the ten miles to the farmers market that sprung up every Saturday on the town square in Clifton Forge.

The family was now long gone. Dead were the parents from natural causes. The children had scattered to follow their dreams of higher education or careers that offered a better life; one that paid much more than a station wagon full of vegetables or a fatted calf sold by the pound. Never did it cross their minds that any of them would return to this cabin. But then again, none of them could ever imagine selling the cabin where they had spent their childhoods and shared so many wonderful memories. Because of this, the cabin continued to deteriorate and be reclaimed by nature.

~2~

The cloud of dust along the dirt road leading to the abandoned cabin announced the arrival of a red MG convertible. With the top down, the dust swirled around the auburn-haired woman behind the wheel. Pulling into the yard, the driver cut the engine. Looking about, the grass reached almost to the top of her door. *I guess the first thing to do is have someone cut the yard.*

Stepping out, her black low-heeled boots were enveloped by the grass. *God I hope there are no snakes. I hate snakes!* Surveying the exterior of her former home, she wondered if she had gone mad. *What in the world made me think moving back here was a good idea? There is no way I can stay here. Not right now.*

Carefully testing each step to ensure it would hold her weight, she made her way to the front door that stood ajar not providing any security for the inside of the home. Stepping inside, her heart sank as she took in the destruction caused by nature, humans and animals. "I have lost my mind completely," announcing the obvious to whatever spirits might be present. "This is going to take a whole lot more money and a whole lot more elbow grease than I thought." A sigh escaped from her as she walked into her former bedroom. Moving from room to room, she realized that the entire house would need to be gutted and practically rebuilt.

During a conference call with her four siblings two months earlier, Susan Leigh had announced that she wanted to move back to the home place and would buy out each of them if they could agree on a price. Phrases such as "you are crazy", "you've lost your mind", "you're going to regret this" answered her announcement. In her heart she believed them to be true, but to start her life anew she needed to escape to a place where she found peace. A place where the pace was slower and she could recover the health she had lost in the rat race of living in D.C. She knew in her heart that going home would be the best medicine. She was just grateful she had not finalized the negotiations with her siblings, convincing them that she needed to visit the home place to determine the amount of work that would be needed to make the home habitable again. *There is no way they will believe how rough this house looks. Pictures will be necessary to make my case.*

Retrieving her phone from her car, she snapped photos of all four sides of the exterior and multiple pictures of each of the interior rooms, making sure she took close ups of the missing plumbing and mold. *This will show them that this house isn't worth anything. It should help me get it for nothing when they see the amount of work that needs to go into making it livable again.*

Pulling the door closed as best she could, Susan returned to her car. Staring at the house, doubt entered her thoughts if she was making the right decision. Starting the car, she backed into the roadway and headed toward town. It was sad to see her home in such deteriorating condition.

~3~

Clifton Forge was a small town nestled in the George Washington National Forest of the Blue Ridge Mountains. Once a booming railroad town, it had become a near ghost town as business after business packed up and moved out after the C&O became CSX and the majority of the jobs followed to Baltimore. The population was aging and the young people were moving to Roanoke or leaving for college, never to return. With the lack of movie theaters or other forms of entertainment, those who stayed got married, had children and then waited to die.

Passing the town line, the sign welcomed visitors to a town that was "scenic, busy and friendly". Susan smiled. She remembered once thinking how succinct and accurate that phrase describing her hometown truly was. There were no strangers in Clifton Forge. Just people you had yet to meet. Passing the dirt lot she and her siblings had driven a homemade go cart on years before and scanning above, she saw her grandparents' two story home standing as a sentinel; watching the traffic coming to and from town. There were many memories in that home, some good, some not so good. The first cemetery on her left was where her parents laid. *Hi*

Mom and Dad. I'll see ya'll later. She then passed the second cemetery where her father's parents laid.

Dropping down into the main part of town it saddened her heart to see the Coca-Cola plant boarded up. Her paternal grandfather had worked there while her maternal grandfather labored on the railroad. Following Main Street she noticed that many of the buildings once empty were now bursting with businesses that catered to tourists; antique shops, outdoor adventure stores and boutiques.

Keswick took her to the west side of Ridgeway Street. *Wow! They've changed the traffic flow again. I remember when Ridgeway was a two-way street. Now it only runs east.* Susan smiled wondering if it was the business people or the whim of the town government that determined the traffic direction.

Parking on Ridgeway, she decided to walk the short distance to the other end. Passing small restaurants, boutiques, an outdoor adventure store and an art center, it was clear that Clifton Forge was coming alive after all these years. *Maybe this is the right move.* She smiled.

The courthouse still sat at the foot of Jefferson Street. *Well, at least something is familiar.* As she made her way back to the west end of Ridgeway Street a sign hanging from the side of a two story brick storefront announced an eatery; Jack Mason's Tavern. Her stomach told her now would be a good time to eat.

The narrow tavern consisted of a long bar that ran from the front to the back on the right wall. Assorted license plates hung along the ceiling as well as across the beams supporting the ceiling. Lending an air of coziness to the tavern, a small fireplace separated the high-top tables occupying the front of the tavern from the upholstered booths filling the back. Susan claimed one of the tall tables against the wall as the bartender greeted her from behind the bar, "Someone will be right with you!"

"Hi! What can I get you to drink?" The barely twenty-one waitress laid a menu on the table in front of Susan along with a napkin rolled around eating utensils.

"Uh, yes. White wine and ice water with lemon. What do you recommend?"

"Well, for our special this afternoon, we have meatloaf with mashed potatoes and gravy. You can get a salad or one of our sides to go with it."

Looking at the menu as the waitress spoke, Susan decided on the fried pickles, the French onion soup and a Caesar salad. "Great. I'll be right back with your drinks."

With the meal finished, Susan decided to take another walk through town. She thought she had noticed an inn on Jefferson Street. *Wonder if they have room at the inn for this solitary pilgrim.* Susan laughed to herself as she compared herself to pilgrims of the past. Taking time to really look at the window displays at the various businesses, they confirmed her suspicions. This town is on the up and coming not the down and out. *Maybe this move will work. I hope so.*

The Red Lantern Inn occupied the old bus station. Entering the front door, Susan noticed the furnishing of the lobby were mostly antiques. The rug on the floor appeared to be a real oriental and the enclosed porch to the left was furnished with assorted wicker chairs and settees. Susan's attention was called to the right side of the entrance when she was greeted by a woman standing behind the counter who confirmed they had a vacancy.

~4~

Staying at The Red Lantern Inn would not only be comfortable but also convenient. Internet was available allowing her to stay in communication with her job and her siblings. Being within walking distance of several restaurants allowed her to not only get exercise but also change her dining options.

Talking with various customers at the tavern and the staff at the hardware store, she was directed to contractors to help with the renovation of the cabin and the maintenance of the yard. The two she called agreed to be there the next day. That meant she would need to be at the cabin first thing in the morning to determine if her dreams could become a reality. She decided to start demolition to help get the show moving. The good news was that her siblings, after viewing the photos of the cabin's condition, agreed to sell her the cabin for the cost of the land; a whopping four thousand dollars.

Eyes followed her as the locals watched the newest stranger in town walking down the street carrying her newly acquired sledgehammer. She could see them whispering to each other as she made her way back to the inn. Smiling to herself, she knew she had been the topic of conversation since she parked her little red MG on Ridgeway Street and stepped out wearing her knee-high boots. This was nothing new to her. She had been the topic of conversation when she was younger.

As a teen, her then flame red hair made her look like Bozo the Clown the time she decided to fro her hair. All the kids at school laughed at her. Well, almost all. Paula, one of the girls in her gym class, said she thought the look was groovy. And one of the boys in the senior class actually asked her to dance at the Sadie Hawkins Day Dance.

Then, when she decided to wear a miniskirt to school with white go-go boots, unbeknownst to her parents, she not only became extremely popular with the boys but she also drew the attention of the administration. Her parents were summoned to the school to bring her a skirt with a more appropriate length. That evening she not only received a whipping but she also went to bed hungry and was restricted for the next two weeks causing her to miss two football games and a dance.

"Susan! Susan Leigh!? Is that you!?" Susan turned to see a tall, leggy brunette walking toward her. Not recognizing her, the woman continued. "Susan, its Becky! Becky Fitzgerald! How are you? It's been so long!" By the time Becky finished her re-introduction, she had reached Susan and wrapped her arms around her, locking Susan's arms at her sides. Susan searched her memory to remember a Becky from her past.

Finally, the light bulb came on just as Becky released her. "Becky! How are you? It's been a long time." Stepping back, Susan's right arm felt so much heavier than her left. Setting the sledgehammer on the sidewalk, she shook her arm to restart the circulation that had been cut off by Becky's hug.

"It sure has. I don't think we've seen each other since graduation."

The two sat through five years of English together and shared a few other classes; the most notable being Biology when they had both been held after class for talking and the teacher, Mr. McCoy, tried to make inappropriate advances toward both of them. He had the reputation of taking advantage of underclassmen, but no one ever had the nerve to report him. Those assigned to Mr. McCoy were grateful for not being assigned the other Biology teacher, Mr. Grizzard, who had a mirror strategically placed in his bottom desk drawer. Known to call female students to his desk under the guise of discussing one of their assignments, he would open his bottom drawer just enough to allow him a view up their skirts.

"Are you in town for a visit?" Becky took Susan's hand. "We must get together. I would love to catch up."

Withdrawing her hand, Susan shared that she would be moving back to town and she would be living at her old home place. "Give me your number and I'll give you a call."

"Well, a lot of people have moved back. I'm one of them. After college I went to LA but came home when my mother got sick. Been almost ten years now," Becky explained.

"It looks like the town fell on hard times for a while, but it looks like it's coming back," Susan observed.

"Yes! It is!" Becky was enthusiastic with her answer. Susan learned that Becky was head of the Tourist Bureau and was instrumental in bringing many businesses back to town. Her goal was to make Clifton Forge a tourist destination for outdoor adventurers, artists, artisans and the culinary elite. "We just obtained a grant for the tavern to open a brewery. It will be located right next door to the tavern and they already have a world class master cicerone onboard."

Checking the time, Susan knew the day was marching on. She needed to get to the cabin to begin demolition. The contractor would arrive tomorrow and she wanted a preview of what he may find behind the walls. "Becky, this is fascinating. I would love to learn more, but I need to go to my parents' cabin. I will definitely give you a call."

"Where are you staying?"

"The Red Lantern Inn." Susan responded.

"Great. We can have lunch or dinner one day. Please. Call me. I would love to tell you about the many opportunities for you to get involved in." Hugging Susan again, "It's so great to see you back in town."

"It's great to be here." Susan knew in her heart that she wasn't just saying that. She believed the run in with Becky was God's confirmation she had made the right move. Picking up her sledgehammer, Susan made her way to her car.

Pulling up to the cabin, she knew daylight was short. Easing up the steps, she attacked one of the walls knocking a hole the size of the hammer head in the wall. A couple more swings sapped the remaining energy from her tiring body. *I'm thinking it's time to call it a day. Tomorrow will bring more time and more sunlight. The drive was maybe more than this tired old body could take.*

Setting the sledgehammer in the corner, Susan decided to return to her room to get some much needed rest.

~5~

The morning sun shone down on the tractor pulling the bush hog a good distance into the field. Thankfully, he had cut the area around the house first. It was still taller than she liked but at least it was a start. Now the grass only reached just above the black of her tire. Surveying the yard, there was a large amount of cut grass laying in clumps. *Wonder if he will get that up with a rake? I hope so.*

Susan slowly mounted the front steps trying to remember where she had placed her feet the day before. Pushing the door open, it resisted her ever so slightly but finally allowed her to enter. Unfortunately, the fairies had not appeared and completed the demolition and construction. *Guess it's up to you and me Lord.* Grabbing the sledgehammer from the corner where she left it the night before, she surveyed the cabin. Walking into her parents' bedroom she decided that would be a great place to start this morning since it was one of the largest rooms.

Lifting the sledgehammer, she swung it back and then forward bouncing it off the wall. *What? I must have hit a two by four.* Swinging again, aiming for another spot, the hammer slammed through the wall causing wallpaper to tear and the supporting plaster to crash to the floor. Pulling the sledgehammer free of the hole, she swung again and again opening a hole about three feet wide and two feet tall.

"I hope you have a gun." The male voice startled her causing her to jump.

Turning to face the voice, she saw the forty something male she had hired to address the grass problem standing in the doorway. Gary had come highly recommended by the manager of the inn and the barkeep at the tavern. "Uh, no. I don't. Why? Do I need one? You must be Gary. I'm Susan. We talked on the phone."

"Nice to meet you. You just might. Could be snakes hold up inside the walls."

The news caused apprehension to fill her. "Do you really think so? How could they get in?"

"Snakes can get into most anywhere." He moved toward her. "All they need is just a small opening to slither through." Having a good four inches on her, his hair was dark brown and his eyes deep sky blue. Muscles were definitely evident under his denim shirt tucked into his well worn jeans which were tucked into his muck boots. The musky smell of his sweat aroused her interest. "If you are going to be opening up walls, you need to have a gun to neutralize whatever comes out."

"So, where can I get one?"

"You'll have to drive to Roanoke for that. There aren't any gun stores in town. Have you ever shot a gun?"

Puffing up, Susan responded. "I have. Daddy used to take us hunting back in the day."

"Well, hunting with a shotgun or a rifle is a lot different than handling a handgun. You'll need to learn to handle one."

"Can you teach me?" Susan set the sledgehammer on the floor. Scanning the room, she tensed thinking snakes now lurked in every corner and crevice. The thought deflated the urge to complete the demolition herself.

"Maybe. Look, I just wanted to let you know that I've finished the field. I'll be back tomorrow with the tedder to scatter the grass. Then I'll rake and bale. Do you want round or square bales?"

"Uh, I don't know. It's been a long time since I was around farming. I've been living in the city for the past few years. Which do you recommend?"

"Square bales. People have horses around here and prefer square bales. You could probably sell them for seven bucks a piece."

"Oh wow." Being pleased with this news, Susan knew the selling of the hay would offset the cost of having it cut and baled. "Ok. Well, square bales then. Do you have any idea how many we'll get?"

Moving toward the door, he stopped. "Well, you have five acres. So, you should get ten to fifteen bales. Maybe more."

"OK. Well, I'll get the gun if you'll help me learn to handle it. Thanks Gary."

He nodded. "No problem." And with that, she heard his foot falls retreat from the house and the engine of his truck turn over.

Susan turned to look at the wall. *Well, I hate snakes but I want to see how bad things are behind the walls.* Grabbing the sledgehammer she swung it toward the wallpaper. Crashing through another section of the wall the head didn't go as deep as it had before. Susan stopped to see what she had hit. Pulling a piece of wall away she saw what appeared to be a bag lodged in the cavity.

Reaching in, Susan felt what could have been canvas. Withdrawing the bag from the cavity, surprise filled her. The bag was definitely canvas. The top was leather with a zipper and what appeared to be a sewn in lock. Once removed, another bag fell. Removing the second bag, a third fell. Retrieving the third there was no fourth bag. She took the sledgehammer and removed the rest of the wall above and below the hole that had spilled the three bags. Nothing else revealed itself. Erring on the side of caution, she then finished demolishing the rest of the cavities on the same wall ensuring that no more bags hid from her.

Taking the bags into what used to be the kitchen, she set them on the counter. Pulling the tab on the first bag, the zipper opened easily even though it had been in the wall for an unknown number of years. The other two bags followed suit.

The contents set Susan back. Money. Lots and lots of money. There were tens, twenties, fifties and hundreds. She opened the second and third bags finding the same. Susan looked around for a chair, but there was none. Sitting on the floor, she took the bags with her. Grateful to be alone during this discovery, she wondered where this money had come from. Each of the bags were embossed with the faded name "Mountain National Bank." Thumbing through the bills it appeared the oldest date she could find was in the nineteen fifties. *Where in the world did this money come from? Did my parents know this money was here? They had to. How else would it get in their bedroom wall? So many questions.*

Zipping up the bags, Susan decided to call it a day here at the cabin. Not bothering to clean up the mess she made, she took the bags and leaving the sledgehammer where she set it in the bedroom, she returned to the inn. *I need a safe place to put these, but I can't let anyone know about this. I need to count the money to know how much is in here.*

Thankfully, the common rooms were unoccupied upon her return to the inn. Susan was able to smuggle the bags in wrapped in her jacket. Mounting the stairs, she made her way to her room. Closing her door, ensuring it was locked to avoid anyone, including the maid, from coming in, she laid the bags on her bed. Lowering the shades and pulling the curtains darkened the room. She switched on the table lamp beside the window and then moved toward the bed. With the bedside lamp illuminated, she had enough light to fully examine the contents of the bags.

One hour later, Susan knew she had one hundred thousand dollars sitting before her. *One hundred thousand dollars! How in the world did my parents get one hundred thousand dollars in cash? We scraped by every single day and there was one hundred thousand dollars sitting in the wall?* Susan became incredulous. A feeling of betrayal filled her. "How could they have all this money and not use it to take care of us?" She voiced to no one. "We had to wear hand-me-downs and patched jeans. We shopped at the discount stores. We could have had so much more." Realizing she was speaking her thoughts aloud, she blushed. *I hope no one heard me.*

Checking the time, she realized the banks were now closed. She had nowhere safe to secure the cash. "I can't leave it here. Someone will steal it. But I'm hungry." Talking to herself, she needed to come up with a way to secure the money until she got to the bank. "I need to meet the contractor first thing tomorrow since he was unable to make it today. I can't just run around town with a hundred thousand dollars in cash on me. Oh geez!"

Calling the contractor, Susan successfully pushed tomorrow's meeting to later in the day allowing her to address her discovery. Looking about her room, she decided the only place she could secure the money was in her suitcase. *I guess that will have to do till tomorrow.*

~6~

The next morning brought a very tired Susan who had tossed and turned unable to sleep. Hearing every little noise made by other guests, and the building itself, convinced her someone was trying to gain entry to her room. She just knew someone knew she had found the money and was trying to get it. Little did she know how right she was.

Walking into Alleghany National Bank, the only bank in town, Susan approached the gentleman sitting behind the desk situated in the corner of the lobby. A desk that appeared to have been there since the bank opened many years before. As he stood and came around the side of the desk she could see that his pants were a couple of inches too short for his bowed legs. His tie was frayed but his jacket appeared new. Extending his pallid hand that appeared to not see much sunlight, he introduced himself as Bill Clark. His slicked back blonde hair exposed a high forehead and accentuated his aquiline nose giving him a hawkish appearance. His brown eyes, surrounded by extremely long lashes and heavy eyebrows, emphasized that hawk likeness. *Why do guys always get the gorgeous lashes?* She smiled to herself.

"Good morning, Mr. Clark. My name is Susan Nicely. I would like to rent a large safe deposit box."

"Why sure Mrs. Nicely. I'll need you to fill out some paperwork and show me your ID." Reaching into his desk drawer he withdrew the necessary forms.

Susan felt as if she was sitting in a fish bowl and anyone who came in would know her business. "Uh, is there somewhere private we could move to? I don't feel very comfortable sitting out here in the open." She looked about.

Surprised at this request, Billy Clark looked about seeking to accommodate her. "Uh, excuse me just a moment." Rising, he walked toward a door to the right of the tellers. Disappearing as he turned left, he soon returned. "We can use the room in the back." Taking the paperwork, he waited for Susan to stand.

~7~

Forty-five minutes later having stashed the bank bags in the largest safe deposit box the bank offered and hitting the fast food drive through for breakfast, Susan headed toward the cabin. Eating and driving, she was careful to watch for deer as she exited the interstate onto route forty-two heading north. The clock on her dash told her she was right on schedule, or maybe even a few minutes early.

Arriving at the cabin, the dark blue Ram pick-up sat in front of the porch. Cliff came from around the back of the house. A smile spread across his face as Susan exited her car, wiping her hands on her jeans.

"Cliff? Cliff Burke?"

"The one and only," he declared as he stepped toward her, wrapping his arms around her giving her a big bear hug.

"You're smushing me!" Susan exclaimed. "Let me go." She laughed.

"It is so good to see you," Cliff declared, "after all these years. Welcome back to the hood."

"It's good to be back, I think." Susan replied. "It looks like life has been good to you."

"Yea, pretty good. I took over my Dad's business after he retired. Been working it ever since."

"That's great. So, who'd you marry?"

"Now what makes you think I'm married?" Cliff grinned.

Embarrassed at her presumption, Susan replied. "Well, I just assumed that since you stayed in town you had to have gotten married. After all, all the girls were hot after you in high school." Susan could see the confidence rise in Cliff.

"True. True. But there was only one girl I had eyes for and she left town, never to return…until now."

That declaration caught Susan off guard. She and Cliff had been buddies in high school. They went to the football games together and had a few drinks together; even hung out under the bridge that supported Ridgeway Street, but she never thought there were any feelings involved. Just friends. Trying to remain aloof and coy, Susan asked who that girl was. "I never knew you had the hots for anyone in high school. I thought you liked playing the field."

"I played the field because the one girl I wanted had no idea and I didn't want to ruin a great friendship."

Susan knew he was talking about her. "Well, we'll just have to find that girl and let her know how you felt." Smiling she headed toward the cabin. "Now, let's see what we need to do to make this place livable again."

Following behind, Cliff replied, "Yea, let's see." Walking behind, he enjoyed the view as her hips swayed back and forth as she walked.

Slowing to take caution as she mounted the steps, she approached the door. Gingerly opening it, she stepped in.

~8~

Two hours later they stood in the yard again. Both agreed that it would be best that the house be completely demolished. Cliff convinced her to have the house built on pylons to mitigate flooding. He showed her data indicating the house had been flooded since her family had vacated years before and it would be subject to more flooding if the wet weather pattern remained the same. Melancholy filled her at the thought of completely losing the entire house. "Are there any features of the house that can be saved? It breaks my heart that everything will just be gone with no remnant of what was."

"Well, we could salvage some of that flowered wallpaper," he grinned.

"Funny," she didn't smile.

"Let's go back in and see what we can reasonably salvage."

Following him back into the house, Susan really wanted something to keep some aspect of the house; something to keep her parents' spirit around.

"Ok," Cliff began. "You said you wanted to keep the fireplace. Or at least have a fireplace in the new place."

"Yes," Susan agreed. "But how can we take part of the house and insert it into the fireplace?"

"Well, we could salvage the bricks used in this fireplace and use them in the new. If we don't have enough, we can always get more to match," Cliff looked at Susan seeking approval.

"How can you possibly match bricks that are more than fifty years old?" Susan doubted what Cliff proposed.

"It's done all the time," he declared. "There have been a lot of folks moving down here from Northern Virginia. They reclaim these dilapidated houses out in the country…"

"Kinda like what I'm doing?" Susan interrupted.

"Well, yea," Cliff continued. "We find bricks from salvage yards to match all the time. And if we can't, there's a brickyard in Roanoke that can pretty much match any brick we have."

"How are you going to support a fireplace fifteen feet in the air?" Not knowing anything about construction, Susan found it impossible to be able to support a fireplace that far above ground. "I always thought a fireplace had to sit on a concrete platform to give it support and to keep it from sinking into the ground."

"Normally they do," Cliff acknowledged, "but, we have our ways to deliver what our clients want," he grinned. "Now, what I need you to do is meet with an architect to have plans drawn up."

"How long is this going to take?"

"Well, it depends on the schedule of the architect, how long it takes you to meet with him and the county giving you the building permit."

Sighing, "Do you think there will be a problem getting a permit?"

"No. Just tell them what you want. If you want a house bigger than this, you may need a new septic. But, that shouldn't be a problem."

"Great. Ok. Who do ya'll use?"

"Dean, Topping and Driscoll in Roanoke. They do a lot of work in this area. Get your phone, I'll give you their number."

~9~

Driving back into town Susan knew priority one would be to get the house going. The quicker the house was built the quicker she could move in and start living her life. Calling the architectural team Cliff had recommended she made an appointment for tomorrow at eleven. Cliff had shared that he would need to obtain a permit to demolish the house, but that wouldn't happen until the plans for the new house had been approved and he knew what size house and septic would be approved by the county. Susan was grateful for that news. Something was telling her there were more mysteries hidden in the walls of that house. The delay in demolition would give her an opportunity to knock out more walls. Then she would begin her research of where the money came from.

Parking behind the inn, she decided to grab her computer from her room and walk to the tavern. The sun would feel good on her face. Spring was definitely here and the weather could only get better. Sliding into her favorite seat at her favorite table, the bartender called out, "Hi Susan! The usual?"

"Yes. Thanks." *I think I've been eating here way too much.* She laughed to herself. Her usual table with her back to the wall, allowed her to not only view the outside world but also to see who came and went from the tavern. If word got out about the money she would probably become a target for some whack job…maybe a robbery. So, she kept all information about what she had found to herself. Not even sharing with her siblings.

Booting up the computer she went to the Virginia State Library website pulling up their digital resources. She then searched the newspaper archive searching for any articles about Mountain National Bank in Virginia. She then narrowed her search to Virginia prior to the nineteen seventies.

"Hi! What can I get you?" Brad stood before her just on the other side of her computer screen.

"Hi! Brad. How are you?"

Laying a menu and napkin wrapped eating utensils on the table he also set her water with lemon and a glass of white wine. "Well. I take it no one will be joining you this afternoon?"

"Nope." Susan smiled. "Just doing some research."

"So, you want your pickles?" Brad continued.

"That would be nice. Thank you." Susan then went back to her screen as Brad walked away. Her screen now displayed more than thirteen hundred results. She sighed.

Clicking on the image that appeared to be the most promising, a copy of the Daily Review published in nineteen sixty, now filled her screen. *Either I'm going blind or this print is really, really small.* Clicking the plus sign to the right of the screen, she increased the font until she was able to read it. Thankfully, the program had highlighted all of the "mountain", "national" and "bank" words on the page. As she read, Susan learned that there had been a robbery at the Mountain National Bank in Clifton Forge the day before. The robbers never showed a gun, but according to the article, they insinuated they were armed. Three men were involved in the robbery and all three wore hoods over their heads concealing their identities. No arrests were ever made. Saving the article to her desktop, she closed that edition and opened the next. No new news was reported.

"Did you contact the architect?" Jumping, Susan looked up to see Cliff standing in front of her.

"You following me?"

"Nah. Just thought I would get some dinner," Cliff grinned. "Whatcha' doing?"

Closing the laptop, "Nothing."

Sliding into the chair across from her, "Mind if I join you?"

"It looks like you already have," Susan observed as her pickles were delivered to the table.

"Hey Cliff," Brad slid a dark malt beer in front of him. "You want anything to eat?"

Taking a sip of his beer, "not right now." Turning his attention back to Susan, the inquisition began. "So, what brings a big city lawyer like you back to this little one horse town?" He grinned. I thought when you graduated you were out of here and were never coming back."

"I changed my mind," was all Susan offered.

Taking another sip from his beer, Cliff continued to push for an explanation. "You know you might as well tell me why you came home," he grinned. "You know I'll find out eventually."

Susan knew what he said was true. There were no secrets in this town. Even secrets people thought they would take to their grave would re-surface...eventually. "I was having some health problems," she admitted. "The rat race in DC just became too much." Taking a fried pickle from the basket, she dipped it in the ranch dressing and bit the now white end. Chewing, she bought time to decide how much she really wanted to reveal to her old pal.

"Well, I'm sure it can be pretty stressful," Cliff acknowledged. "But, couldn't you get away on week-ends?"

Susan shook her head as she swallowed and then sipped her wine. Speaking quietly she decided to go ahead a spill. "The environment is high pressure up there. You are never really off and week-ends are not your own if you are working several high profile cases. To get away, you have to drive in traffic that is bumper to bumper. Most people metro in and a commute could take up to an hour if you live in the close suburbs. Some people travel as much as two hours one way. I lived in Alexandria, so I was fairly close." She took another sip of her wine. "But, living close in you are constantly barraged with noise and people and social interaction. There is zero down time. So, my body made its own down time." Leaning closer to Cliff, "Please don't share this with anyone." She waited.

"You know I don't gossip."

"I came home late one evening, poured myself a glass of wine, took the wine bottle to the sofa, sat down and didn't emerge from my townhouse for a month." Silence followed Susan's disclosure.

Minutes passed before Cliff spoke. "So, are you ok now?"

"Yes."

Just then Brad returned to take their food order. As he stepped away, taking the empty pickle basket with him, Cliff continued. "What did your boss say? Did anyone miss you?"

Susan smiled. "Yes, my boss was the only one to miss me…and my assistant since my workload fell on her. I didn't take any of their calls. I just sat and watched mindless TV, drank wine and slept. I eventually snapped out of it and decided I didn't want to live like that anymore. So, I went in and tendered my immediate resignation."

Surprise filled Cliff's face, "Oh wow. So you don't have a job?"

Susan laughed. "Don't worry. I have money for the house. And no, I do have a job. Thankfully, my boss liked me and knew the value of my brain, so he agreed to let me work long distance."

"Well that's good."

Susan agreed. "That way, I can stay current on securities and do research. Someone else can deal with the BS in the District."

Turning the conversation to the topic of house construction Susan shared that the new house would be a one story and she had an appointment with the architect the next morning.

The evening wasn't nearly as productive as Susan had wished after Cliff arrived. Finishing her meal, she decided to return to the inn where she would have some privacy and could get something accomplished.

Logging back into the library website she continued her newspaper search. There were several articles about the robbery but none disclosed how much was taken. *Hum. Wonder how I can find out without calling attention to my interest.* Search as she might, she never found any articles announcing an arrest. *Interesting.*

~10~

"How's it goin' Sis?" The familiar voice came across her speaker.

"Dewey! What a pleasant surprise!" Dewey was Susan's favorite brother; probably because they were only a year apart. She followed him like an unshakable shadow until he went to high school. Then, when she arrived herself, he told her to never acknowledge him at school under the pain of death. She knew he was joking. At least she thought he was, but she never wanted to test him. So, doing as he ordered, she watched him from afar until she developed her own circle of friends. "It's going," she replied. "Slow, but steady. I met with the contractor…"

"Yeah. I know." Dewey interrupted.

"You know?" Susan was surprised. "You spyin' on me?"

"Nah. Cliff called and let me know he was working for you to build a new house. Wow! That house must be in worse shape than the pictures showed. You got the money to do this?"

With her thoughts turning to the bags she found in the wall, "Yea, I got the money. If I run short I'll just borrow some."

"How long you gonna be there? Thought I might come in and give you a hand." Dewey really just wanted to see the old home place before it was demolished and replaced with something spanking new and probably modern.

Appreciating the offer, Susan was hesitant to have her brother join her. Not having decided if she would share the find with her siblings, or if it was even hers to share, she really wanted to keep the secret to herself for now. "I'll probably only be here a couple more days. I really need to get stuff done at home. You know. Close out that life and all."

Pushing, Dewey began to lay down his case for coming to visit. "Well, I can be there tomorrow. I'd really like to see the old place before it's lost to the past. I'll be there around noon or two." Click. The call disconnected.

"Well, that went well." Susan looked at the phone. *I guess I'm getting company. Well. Guess I need to get him a room at the inn.*

Logging off yet again, she made her way downstairs to the desk. "Hi Kathy." Kathy turned allowing Susan to see she was on the phone. Susan waited.

Disconnecting the call, Kathy greeted Susan, "Well, I see you are getting company tomorrow." She announced.

"How did you know?" The disclosure surprised her.

"That was your brother. He said he'll be here around noon tomorrow," Kathy announced.

35

"Do you have room for him?" The number of guests had increased since Susan's arrival. She definitely didn't want to share her room with him.

Smiling Kathy assured her there was room at the inn. I'll put him right next door to you so you'll have connecting doors.

"Oh, you really don't need to go to that much trouble," Susan insisted and hoped to get her point across that she didn't want her brother that close.

Walking back to the kitchen Kathy, with Susan in tow, insisted that it was no trouble at all and how great it would be for them to be so close. Realizing that no amount of persuasion would cause Kathy to change the room assignment, she accepted one of the glasses of merlot Kathy had poured. "Why not join me on the veranda?" Kathy suggested.

Watching the occasional car pass on Jefferson Street, Susan felt she had been invited to an inquisition. Not being from Clifton Forge, Kathy felt compelled to meet as many of the citizens of the small town; present, past and future. The questions ranged from why are you coming back to our fair town to what was it like living in Clifton Forge back in the day.

Susan was happy to reminisce about the town she knew so well; the trips to Douthat catching salamanders and bringing them home to swim in the Cow Pasture and movies at the Masonic Theatre. She talked about riding bikes with her cousins down the hill on Lafayette Street, laughing that it was a miracle none of them were ever run over. "We crossed every intersection without a lookout for oncoming cars," she laughed. "We would finally come to a stop in the gravel parking lot across Commercial Street. Susan even shared the shenanigans of teasing the neighbor next to her grandparents' house and receiving Bazooka bubble gum from the man who lived on Ingalls Street on the Heights. "It was a great childhood. We were always doing something."

"So what makes you want to return?" Kathy prodded. She had retrieved the wine bottle from the kitchen.

Not wishing to share the status of her current health problems that, frankly, no one understands, Susan decided to respond with a sanitized version of her reasons. "I think it's time to slow down a bit. The pace of Northern Virginia is stressful and the cost of living is very expensive. I don't want to sit in traffic anymore to get anywhere." Kathy nodded and Susan continued. "I don't want to meet deadlines anymore. I want to slow down, to have real conversations with people and watch the sun set or rise. I'm blessed that I'm able to have a place…well, will have a place…to come to that is outside of town. I'm blessed I'll be able to hear the Cow Pasture River from my deck or even my bedroom window." She laughed. "I could go on and on, but the point is, I just want to slow down."

"Well, you picked a great time to return. Businesses are coming back and the arts have a great foothold in the area.

Tourists are coming in and there are lots of opportunities for new businesses."

"I agree and I can't wait to become a part of the community." Looking at her phone, Susan realized it was getting late. "Well, I need to call it a night. I have a meeting in Roanoke tomorrow and then prepare for my brother."

Kathy stood as well. "Well, welcome home Susan. I know you'll love it here. Stay with us for as long as you need."

Susan gave her a hug. "Thank you."

~11~

The ride to and from Roanoke was relaxing with beautiful vistas until she arrived in downtown Roanoke. Luckily, the hour of her appointment allowed her to avoid rush hour traffic. Returning to Clifton Forge, she decided to go straight to the cabin. If Dewey was coming into town today, she needed to demolish as many walls as possible to ensure no more bank bags made their appearance. Checking her dash clock, it was already two o'clock. She had a feeling he was already at the inn. *Hopefully he will stay there until I return.*

Approaching the cabin she saw a fire engine red truck sitting in the yard beside the front porch. Gary waved to her as she drove past the field where he was raking the grass cut several days before. *I guess he'll be baling soon.* Pulling up beside the unknown truck Susan assumed it belonged to one of Cliff's workers.

"It's about time you got here!" Susan recognized the voice that admonished her tardiness.

Exiting her MG, she tensed. "What are you doing here?"

Coming down the steps, Dewey reminded her that he told her he was coming. "Yes, I know you did. But I thought you would go straight to the inn."

"I did. But you weren't there. So, I came here and you weren't here either." He wrapped his arms around her. "It's good to see you. How you doin'?"

"Well. I'm here now." She smiled. "I'm doin' good. I see you've been inside?"

"Yea. What a mess. So what's the plan?" Grabbing her arm, he pulled her up the steps, across the porch and into the cabin disregarding the possibility that either could fall through the weather-weakened porch deck.

"Well, let me give you the tour." Pulling her arm from his grip, Susan moved toward the fireplace. "Well, to start, the entire house has to be demolished. But, the good news, we are going to save the bricks from the fireplace and use them in the new house."

"That's good," Dewey approved.

"They are basically going to rebuild the house the way it is, but it's going to be raised up on pylons to avoid flooding. A large deck will be built on the back and screened in." Dewey walked around the house examining the various rooms and returned to the living room with sledgehammer in hand.

"You been taking out some frustrations?" He laughed.

"It's very therapeutic," Susan grinned. "You should try it."

At that suggestion, Dewey walked toward one of the living room walls, lifted the sledgehammer and gave the wall a whack. The head entered the cavity and hung as it slipped down slightly behind the intact wall. Pulling the head toward him he managed to pull a section of wall away that fell to the floor. Swinging again, he continued to smash larger portions than Susan had with her swings. "This is VERY therapeutic," he declared. Continuing the therapy, he swung again, this time catching the head inside the cavity. Pulling the head of the hammer, another portion of the wall fell and with it another canvas bag. "What is this?" Dewey moved toward the section of demolished wall. Susan knew exactly what it was.

Picking up the bag, Dewey turned it over in his hands. "Mountain National Bank? Wasn't that the bank down on Ridgeway when we were kids?" Susan couldn't speak. She just stood there as if frozen. "You ok?"

Stammering, Susan wasn't sure what to say. "Uh, uh, yea. Uh, it was on Ridgeway. I don't think its there anymore." *What are the chances of him finding another bag? How many more bags are in here?* Becoming weak in the knees, Susan sat on the floor.

Repeating his question, "You ok?" Dewey sat down beside her, bringing the bag with him. He could see his sister was as pale as a ghost.

Wiping her forehead, Susan finally responded. "Yea. I'm fine. Open the bag."

Dewey's eyes grew wide as he saw the bag's contents. Bills. Lots of bills. Fives, tens and twenties. Susan said nothing. Pulling the bills from the bag, Dewey separated them into denomination piles. Not believing what he was seeing, he rose. Grabbing the sledgehammer again he began to open the walls that had remained closed after Susan's initial discovery. By the time he had finished, not a closed wall remained and not another bag revealed itself. A fog of dust filled the air. His shirt was moist from sweat and Susan had stepped out on the front porch to fill her lungs with fresh air. Dewey soon joined her. "The only place I can't get is in the kitchen. The cabinets are in the way."

Turning to face him, Susan began, "I need to tell you something." Dewey said nothing. He just looked at her. "I have another hundred thousand sitting in a safe deposit box in town."

"What?" Not believing his ears, the one word question was all he could say.

Susan repeated her statement. Just then they saw Gary's truck approaching the porch. Disappearing inside, Dewey grabbed the piles of money and stuffed the bills back into the bag. *We don't need anyone knowing what we found.* Stuffing the bag into his waistband under his shirt at the small of his back he rejoined Susan on the porch.

"Hey Susan, just wanted to let you know, I'll be baling hay tomorrow and found someone who will buy it."

"Great. Thanks Gary. Can you handle it for me? I would appreciate it."

"Sure. No problem." Gary looked questioningly at the auburn-haired man standing beside Susan and topping her by at least four inches. It was clear from his physique; the guy didn't work out with weights regularly, but his appearance said distance runner. Perceiving that introductions would not be made, he left.

The look Dewey gave her spoke volumes. "Let's go." She directed.

"No." Not moving, Dewey stood his ground. He always did when he was serious about something and wanted to know every last detail. "I'm not going anywhere until you tell me about this money."

"I don't know anything about this money." He could tell she wasn't being completely honest.

"Spill." Sitting on the porch steps, he waited.

Reluctantly Susan sat beside him. She knew it was no use to withhold anything from him. He always figured things out. So she began.

~12~

Dewey had no words once Susan finished her explanation of the money bag including the three bags she had already deposited in the safe deposit box at the bank. Silence filled the air as she waited for him to speak. So many questions raced through his mind, he didn't know where to start. She waited.

"So, was there a bank robbery or something?" Susan had not shared the research she had started.

"Yes." Retrieving her laptop from her car, she booted it up and opened the one article she had saved to her desktop. "I found this in some old newspapers online."

Turning the laptop so he could read the article, Dewey tried to enlarge the screen. Doing so only made the image blurry. "Can you print this out? Or do you have a program that will enlarge without blurring?" Frustration filled his voice.

Taking the computer, she struck keys and opened her Photoshop program. She then opened the picture containing the newspaper article. Enlarging the picture to two hundred percent, she then turned the laptop back to her brother. "Here."

Dewey read. "Local Bank Robbed. Robbers vanish." He looked at Susan. She waited. As he continued to read, his eyes became wider. Once he had finished he declared, "I had no idea this ever happened."

"Well how could you? You were only six. I was five. We didn't read the paper way back then." She laughed.

"So, is this the money from that robbery?" He hoped the answer was no. If it was, how did it get in their house? Behind the walls?

Shaking her head no, all Susan could do was surmise. "I don't know. I read several articles after this one and none of them gave an amount stolen or if there were any arrests."

"This site you're using. Does it have all the newspapers ever published?" He just knew there had to be an article with more information.

"I don't think so. It's through the State Library website and I think it's just a small portion of what was published."

"Well, we need to get copies of all the papers printed back then."

"How do you plan to do that, genius?" Despite the predicament they were in, she still felt the need to needle her brother. After all, if she didn't he would think she was sick…or scared.

Dewey flicked her on her shoulder. "I'm going down to the newspaper and get copies, Mutt." Mutt was the name Dewey had called her as a kid because he said she was like a mutt dog that followed him everywhere.

Flicking him back, Susan announced that the newspaper had merged with the Covington paper and no longer existed.

"Well, I bet they kept copies. We'll go down tomorrow after we go to the bank and just see." Producing the grin on his face he always wore when he knew he was right, Dewey flicked his sister again.

"Stop!" She laughed. "We aren't kids anymore and I'm no mutt."

"Well, you'll always be my mutt!" Laughing he pulled her off the porch and gave her a great big bear hug. "Come on Mutt. Let's go see what's to eat in this little town of ours."

~13~

The tavern was standing room only when they arrived. Live acoustical music greeted them as they entered. "You wanna drink?" Dewey grabbed her arm pulling her through the crowd to the bar.

"Sure. If you're buying."

"Dewey! Susan!" Susan turned to see Cliff sitting at her favorite table. He signaled for them to join him. Acknowledging him, Susan got Dewey's attention and pointed toward Cliff.

"Get me a merlot and meet me there." Without waiting for an answer, she disappeared into the crowd headed toward her favorite table.

As the night wore on, beer and wine flowed and dishes of food came and went. Reminiscing, they laughed until they were in tears over some of their youthful antics. "You know, we should have been in jail," Dewey declared. They all agreed. Bob Dylan, The Beatles and Bob Marley all serenaded their stories. At one point the performer broke into "American Pie" and the entire bar joined in. Before they knew it, it was closing time and last call had been announced. Susan slipped off of her chair and lamented that she and

Dewey should be going. "We have an early morning tomorrow."

"Yea, me too," Cliff declared. "Got a house I'm finishing and then we'll get started on yours if the permits and drawings are back soon."

She nodded. "They should be and the permits shouldn't be a problem. It's going to be basically the same house with just a few floor plan changes. Should go smoothly."

"Great!" Sliding off his chair and moving around to Susan, he gave her a bear hug and shook Dewey's hand while he did. "Take care of Mutt," he admonished Dewey. With that she smacked him on his shoulder.

"I'm no mutt!" She declared and headed for the door. Dewey and Cliff roared with laughter and followed behind. Reaching the sidewalk they said their good-byes. Cliff headed west further up Ridgeway to his truck, Dewey and Susan walked east toward their beds.

Walking down Ridgeway Street the silence between them was almost uncomfortable. The occasional laughter from those leaving the tavern after them followed them down the street. Buildings on either side of the roadway stood darkened and silent; watching them as they ambled toward the inn. Streetlights illuminated their path and the occasional screeching of railroad-car wheels called out to them.

"This was a great town to grow up in," Dewey declared.

"Yes, it was," Susan agreed. "Remember the times at the theatre? We had so much fun."

"Hey. Where exactly was this Mountain National Bank? I don't remember." Dewey stopped as they reached the corner of Ridgeway and Commercial Streets.

Turning to face across Ridgeway, Susan pointed to the Arts Center. "Well, THAT used to be the Leggett's store. Remember?"

"Yea."

"And right beside it was the bank." Susan pointed directly across from where they were standing.

"Wasn't this Zimmerman's?" Dewey pointed to the building they were standing in front of.

Nodding her head yes, Susan confirmed. "And that was Kostel's restaurant." She pointed to the building beside the former bank.

Laughing Dewey looked at her. "Remember when the kids from Tech came over and put bubble bath in the bank fountain?"

"Oh yes," she laughed. "THAT was hilarious!" Both laughing they continued on to their rooms knowing that tomorrow they had a lot to do. First the bank, then the newspaper, then back to the cabin to pull out the cabinets in the kitchen.

"Good night Mutt! Sleep tight. Don't let the bed bugs bite." He laughed as he entered his room and she hers.

~14~

Adding Dewey to the safe deposit box was just a matter of signatures and showing his identification. Once inside the private room, Susan showed him the other bags leaving him speechless. "I know," Susan confirmed his unspoken thoughts. Securing the money in the box, they left the bank in disbelief to what they now had. One hundred and fifty thousand unexplained dollars.

Arriving at the office for the Virginian Review, they were greeted by a perky receptionist sitting at the front desk. "Morning. Can I help ya'll?" Her dark brown eyes and light brown hair was typical of the majority of the citizens of the region. She appeared very knowledgeable about the paper as Susan took the lead in telling her what they where looking for. "Oh. I'm sorry. We don't have any editions of the Daily Review that far back." She sounded very sincere. "But, maybe you can check the historical society or the genealogical society. They may have kept copies."

Disappointed, Susan pressed on. "Thanks. Where would they be?"

"Well, the historical society is on Maple Avenue and the genealogy society is over on Pine Street. I'll get the real addresses and the phone numbers." Rising, she went to the back.

Susan turned to her brother. "Which you want to try first?"

Thinking for a second, he responded, "I think the genealogical society would be our best bet. They probably have a bunch of newspapers." Just then, the receptionist returned handing Susan a piece of paper.

"I'm not sure what their hours are. You might want to give them a call."

"Thanks, you've been very helpful."

Sitting in Dewey's truck Susan called the genealogical society first. The recording informed her they were only open three days a week from ten until three and today was not one of those days. Sighing, she disconnected the call and dialed the historical society. "They aren't open today." Listening to the historical society recording she pressed zero to speak with whoever would answer the phone. After a short conversation Susan learned her best bet would be the genealogical society or actually going to the Virginia State Library in Richmond. The helpful archivist informed her they did not maintain newspapers in bulk and relied on the state library for all of their research.

Thanking her, Susan disconnected the call. "We're batting zero today. The historical society doesn't maintain newspapers. She suggested the state library in Richmond."

"Ok. Well, to the cabin we go." Starting up the truck, Dewey backed out of the parking spot and headed east toward the cabin. "At least we can get the cabinets pulled out."

"You got any tools besides the sledgehammer?"

"Uh, no," he looked at her. "Do you?"

"Do I look like I have tools?" Susan laughed.

"I guess we'll need to stop by the hardware store."

"Guess so."

By the end of the day, all of the cabinets sat in the middle of the former living room. Every wall was opened and dust and debris lay everywhere. Not a single bank bag revealed itself. "Well, I guess we got it all," Dewey observed.

"Unless there are more under the floorboards."

The look on Dewey's face at that very suggestion was priceless. It was a combination of defeat and dread. "So, are you paying Cliff to demolish the house?" He grinned.

Looking at him sideways, Susan confirmed she was, "Do you want him or his workers to find any remaining bags?"

"No."

"Well, then we pull up floorboards."

"Hold up. We don't need to pull up the floorboards. There should be nothing but open floor joists under the house. I'll just look up under there and if I see any place that is covered in boards, we'll just pull up that area…not the whole freaking floor."

Susan agreed. Relieved he had thought of a solution that never crossed her mind. "What about the attic? We gotta check the attic."

"We need a ladder. I'll call Cliff and get him to bring us a ladder...unless you want to buy one of those too," he grinned. "I mean, we already have a crowbar, hammer and sledgehammer. What's a ladder in your tool box?" He laughed.

Frustrated, Susan walked over and smacked Dewey's shoulder. "Do you really want to bring Cliff into this? How you gonna explain needing a ladder?" Susan couldn't believe what she was hearing. "Don't you think he would wonder after all these years why we are just getting around to cleaning out the attic? I mean really. Don't you think we would have done this long before the house got in this condition?"

Frustration was voiced in Dewey's next sentence. "Well, what do you suggest?"

"Well. Let's just tell him we want to take the weathervane off the house."

"Genius! I didn't know it was still up there." Dewey did a little dance.

"Come on. I'm tired. I'm dusty and I want a hot soaking bath...and a glass of wine or three." Susan headed for the door. Dewey followed.

~15~

Sitting amongst the trees on the south side of the Cow Pasture River, she stared through her binoculars watching the demolition. Occasionally one of the siblings would come out onto the back porch covered in dust seeking fresh air. She had roamed these hills as a young girl and knew them as well as she knew her own neighborhood. *They should have known you can't keep a secret in a small town. People talk.*

Ever since she had run into Susan in town, Becky thought it strange she would be moving back home. After all, at graduation she had announced she was knocking the dust of this one horse town off of her and never looking back. Becky had thought Susan arrogant then and her refusal to meet her for even a drink just reinforced her arrogance.

The talk around town, and she remembered around her house, had lent itself that Mr. Nicely, Susan's dad, and two other men had been involved in a bank robbery but police were never able to make a case. Even the money was never found. Becky never heard who the other two men were supposed to be. Drinks with Gary the other evening piqued her interest of what was going on at the house. He had shared that Billy had told him Susan and Dewey had rented a large safe deposit box. Gary shared he thought the timing interesting so soon after the demolition of some of the interior walls. Becky thought it odd since she had heard Cliff was going to tear down the house and build a new one.

Watching the progress, Dewey and Susan were now working on the kitchen cabinets. *They must be looking for something.* Becky observed to herself. *Why else would they be destroying the interior of the house?* She continued to watch. The rustling of bushes and the snap of twigs broke her concentration. Looking about she saw no one. *Must be a critter.* The noise did not scare her. She was at home in these woods.

"Whatcha lookin' at?" The voice made her jump. Turning around she found Gary not five feet from her. "You've lost your edge, little girl." He grinned.

"No I've not. I just figured it was a critter. Sit down." She then turned back to watch the demolition. Just then she saw Dewey entering the crawl space. "They've got to be looking for something."

"I think its money," Gary observed.

Lowering the binoculars from her eyes, she looked at Gary. "Why do you say that?"

"Why else would they be destroying the house? They've hired Cliff and he told me he was going to start demolition as soon as she gets the plans for construction."

"Well, looks like they can't wait for him." The two watched in silence as Dewey came back out from under the house. Susan was sitting on the back porch waiting for him.

From the body language of the siblings, it appeared that whatever he was looking for under the house wasn't there. They then went back into the house closing it up. The only vehicle parked out front left.

Standing, Becky turned to Gary, "Wanna go for a visit?" She grinned.

"Sure."

They made their way back to the swinging bridge and then crossed the river. Walking down the dirt roadway past their vehicles, they approached the shell of a house. Access was still easy as the doors had no operating locks and several of the windows were broken out.

"Be careful going up the steps." Gary warned.

With the setting sun, shadows grew long across the floor. They could not believe their eyes. Every wall in the house had been destroyed. The kitchen cabinets had been either pulled away from, or off, the wall and sat in the former living room. Wall debris covered the floor making it difficult to walk about. Moving from room to room, it looked like a bomb had been detonated inside.

"Wonder if they've been in the attic yet?"

"I doubt it," Gary responded. "There is no ladder and I haven't seen one on Dewey's truck. There's no way Susan could get one in her little car."

"Do you have one?"

Gary headed for the door. "Be right back."

The tour of the attic seemed to be a waste of time. Nothing was hidden in plain view. Using the light on his phone, Gary went from one end of the house to the other.

"See anything?" Becky had popped her head through the access door wanting to take a look herself.

"Nope. Nothing."

"What about under the insulation?" She had risen to waist high in the opening.

"Well, you can see for yourself, there ain't much up here." Gary swept his arm in the air as if presenting a prize on a game show. "And I'm not in the mood to itch."

"You won't itch, much," she grinned. Stepping into the attic, she was careful to stand on the ceiling joists.

"You're gonna be itching if you start moving insulation without gloves."

"I'll take my chances," she grinned as she started to gently move insulation. Making her way down the joists she gently lifted each section shining her phone light underneath. Gary watched. He had no desire to itch.

By the time she had finished half of the attic, Gary decided to pitch in to speed up progress. He had no desire to be in the attic, or even in the house, after dark. By the time they came back down the ladder, they were both itching and the search had been fruitless.

Pulling the ladder from the access hole after replacing the cover, Gary carried it out to his truck. The sun had sunk below the mountains with the last of the day's rays reaching into the darkening sky. The first stars were peaking out from the darkness to the east.

"Well, at least we know they have either found whatever they're lookin' for or there is nothing here to find," Becky observed.

Opening his driver's door, Gary instructed Becky to get in the truck. "I'll give you a ride to your car."

"That's ok. I'll walk." Becky started toward her car.

Insisting, Gary observed that the darkness was coming fast and she didn't know what lurked between here and her car. "I know you're comfortable in the wild, but you never know what's coming down off the mountain. Get in."

Agreeing with his argument Becky got in the truck. "Thanks for your help." She always thought Gary was handsome. Just a couple years younger than her, she never thought he ever noticed her. "So, what made you show up across the river this afternoon?"

Pulling up beside her car, he turned to her. "I've heard the talk too. And I know you never really liked Susan. So, when I saw you talking to Billy Clark at the bank, I knew you would be snooping around."

"Snoop! I don't snoop!" Becky became indignant.

Gary laughed. "What do you call sitting across the river looking through binoculars?"

"Well. I guess you got me there," she laughed. "Wait! How did you know I was talking to Billy?"

"I bank there too ya know. It's the only bank in town. I'm not driving to Covington to do my banking when I live up in Millboro Springs."

Sitting back in the seat, "Oh. Ok. That's reasonable." Thinking for a minute, she continued. "So, do you think they are looking, or were looking, for the money?"

"You talking about the bank robbery money from back in the day? Gosh. I don't know. How would they know to? They've been gone from town since they graduated from high school. I didn't hear about the bank robbery rumor until long after high school. How would they know?"

"I don't know. Maybe their dad told them before he died?"

"So you believe he robbed the bank?" Gary looked at her.

Becoming defensive Becky turned to face him, "Don't you?"

"It's just talk. Whatever happened way back then, we don't know. We were really, really young."

Becky could see that Gary was becoming uncomfortable with the conversation. "Ok. I'm heading home. Thanks for your help." Exiting the truck, she then followed him to the main road. He turned right for home, she left back to town.

~16~

Six weeks later after many conversations with the architect and contractor, the plans were approved, permits issued and demolition had been completed. The lot where her house had stood was just that, an empty lot.

Susan and Dewey had returned to their respective homes after finding no clues about the robbery of the bank. Submitting her resignation again, her boss talked her into remaining with the law firm and continuing as a remote research attorney. She was eager to accept the offer to keep funds coming into her bank account, not knowing when she would find work in her new hometown.

Checking back into the inn, Susan reclaimed her old room telling Kathy she would be there until her new home was completed. "Well, honey, you are welcome to stay as long as you need." Susan thanked her.

"Maybe we can enjoy a glass of wine or two and you can bring me up to speed on the ins and outs of this town," Susan smiled.

"Of course. Of course. If you would like."

Grabbing her bags, Susan looked at Kathy, "Can we start tonight?"

"Sure. Why don't we start at the tavern?"

~17~

Schooling began at five o'clock sharp. Kathy had explained that it would be best to be in position by then. "After all, people are getting off work at that time and Thursday night is a good night at the bar. They have live music and karaoke between sets," she laughed. "Just the experience would be an education, but I can give you the low down on everyone who comes in." Sitting at the high table in the front corner of the tavern, they had a perfect view of everyone who came and went as well as those walking up and down Ridgeway.

As the evening wore on, the drinks flowed, food came and went and the edification of Susan was in full swing. She learned who was divorced, who was running around on their significant other, who had embezzled funds and who had served time along with their assorted offenses. Susan learned that outsiders had come into town buying up various properties and ingratiating themselves into the powers that be. This allowed them to obtain permits that others may not be able to obtain. As time wore on, the true colors of these same outsiders revealed themselves and their funds weren't as limitless as originally proclaimed. As a result, many of these buildings, either residences or commercial buildings they promised to rehab, still stood boarded up.

Susan shook her head. "Well, the more things change, the more they stay the same."

Kathy agreed. "It's truly sad. This town has so much potential." Finishing her glass of wine Kathy suggested they take a walk.

Checking the time, Susan hadn't realized how late the night had become. "Wow. Time really passed. Ok. Let's walk."

Turning west on Ridgeway Kathy headed toward Roxbury Street. "Aren't you going the wrong way?"

"I want to show you something." Kathy responded. "Plus, I'd like to talk with you about something.

Turning east on Keswick they made their way toward Main Street. Stopping in front of some of the boarded up houses, Kathy began. "These are some of the houses I was referring to. They were purchased by a blue blood out of Richmond promising to make them shining examples of what could be. Unfortunately, these same houses are now in foreclosure. How would you like a deal?"

Laughing Susan thought Kathy had lost her mind. "Uh, I already have my hands full with the construction. Besides, I don't have the money."

"You could use some of the money in your safe deposit box."

Stopping in her tracks and grabbing Kathy's elbow, she turned to face her. "How did you know about the money?"

"There are no secrets in this town. Didn't you learn anything during your lesson tonight?"

Speechless, Susan stared at her. Minutes passed before she regained her composure and her voice. "Where did you hear this?"

"Well, don't you have money in the safe deposit box?"

"I can neither confirm nor deny."

"You just did by your reaction," Kathy laughed.

Frustrated, Susan could not believe what she heard. "Well, smarty pants, how much is in the box?"

"I haven't heard the exact amount, but word on the street is that its north of a hundred thousand."

Livid, Susan, again, was unable to speak.

Seeking to calm Susan, she continued. "Look. The guy you dealt with at the bank cannot keep a secret. He tells everything he knows."

"But how did he know what I put in the box?"

"There has been a rumor going around for years he has a duplicate set of customer keys. Word is that he goes into boxes just to see what is in there. I've never heard if he takes anything."

Not believing what she was hearing, Susan just listened.

"Since there is no camera in the room, they've never been able to confirm this rumor. I wish I had known you were going to the bank."

Finding her voice, Susan responded. "Why?"

"Because I would have warned you about the rumor and told you to find another bank."

"Well, I guess it's too late," Susan sighed.

Turning to walk toward Main Street and the inn, Kathy continued. "I also understand you're researching an old bank robbery." She decided she might as well spill everything.

Stopping again, Susan couldn't believe what she was hearing. "Oh my gosh! Do you know everything about me?"

Kathy shrugged. "Only what I've heard from you and the rumors."

Wondering if she had made a major mistake moving back to Clifton Forge, she had nothing more to say until they reached the inn. The silence between them was palpable; occasionally interrupted by a passing vehicle or the distant sound of people talking or laughing. Doubts filled her being. "Well, thanks for the disclosures, Kathy. If you hear anything else about me, please let me know."

Hugging her, Kathy assured her that she would. "Look, you're the new kid in town. As soon as someone else moves in, they'll be the talk of the town."

"Well, I hope someone new moves in quick. Goodnight." With that, Susan mounted the stairs to her room. Closing the door behind her, she laid across the bed staring at the ceiling. The lights from the library parking lot gave little illumination in her room, but she chose to embrace the darkness of the room that matched the current darkness of her spirit. "Oh me," she sighed quietly.

~18~

Morning came early. Light coming through the windows danced across her eyes waking her. Using her hands to shade her eyes, she looked at the clock on the nightstand. Six a.m. *Oh me. What do I do today? If Billy Clark has keys to the boxes, how do I know if he hasn't removed any money? It's been sitting there for more than two months and I thought it was safe. Guess I need to go to the bank.* Rising, she showered and went for breakfast.

As the clock tower struck nine Billy unlocked the lobby door and Susan stepped through. "I'd like to go to my safe deposit box," she announced. *Am I suspicious or did a panicked look enter his eyes? Well, if anything is missing, he should panic.*

With the door closed behind her, she opened her box to find the four bank bags still there. Sitting at the table, she emptied each bag stacking the money in denomination piles. Separating those piles into individual piles of five hundred dollars each, she counted; one hundred and forty thousand dollars. *What?* Counting again, she still came up with one hundred and forty thousand dollars. *I'm missing ten thousand dollars! I know there was a hundred and fifty thousand in these bags!* Counting the money again she found that it was still just one hundred and forty thousand dollars. *That bastard stole ten thousand dollars!*

Putting the money back in the bags, she then stashed them in her oversized purse. Closing the box, she returned to the gate and signaled to Billy that she was finished.

With the money in the seat beside her she headed east over North Mountain. Dialing Dewey's number, she sought his advice of what to do. *Do I report this theft or do I wait?*

After listening to what Susan had been told by Kathy and then the disclosure of the missing ten grand, Dewey tried to calm her down and get her to think. "If you report the theft, they are going to want to see the money. If that money is stolen, you've lost it all."

"I know, but that bastard isn't getting away with stealing my money!" Susan insisted.

Your money? Dewey let it pass. "Look. We don't know where the money came from. We need to find out if it was from the bank robbery or if mom and dad were just frugal."

Agreeing, Susan began to calm down. "So, what do I do with the money?"

"Where is it now? Did you leave it in the box?"

"No. It's in my bag." It struck Susan what a knee jerk reaction she had had when she discovered the money missing. *But I'm not going to give him the opportunity to steal more.*

Dewey could not believe his normally very intelligent sister was running around the mountains of Virginia carrying a hundred and forty thousand in cash in her purse. "Alright, listen, head to Staunton and put the money in a safe deposit box there."

"What about Lexington? I'm at the Lexington exit now."

"Too small a town. Scratch Staunton. Go to Roanoke." Dewey directed.

"Why there?"

Growing frustrated he explained. "Larger than Lexington and Staunton. Closer than Charlottesville."

"Ok. When you coming back to Clifton Forge? They finished the demolition and have started on the pylons. They should be starting on the house in a couple weeks."

"I'll call you and let you know. Call me after you deposit the money." With that he disconnected the call and Susan took the I-81 exit toward Roanoke.

~19~

"The money is gone," he declared. She stopped mid-chew.

It was a warm sunny day for a picnic at Douthat. He had left the bank just before noon not wanting to draw suspicion to his activities. Having checked the box after Susan left, he discovered the money was gone. He knew he had to tell Becky but not risk the chance of being overheard at the bank. So, there they sat at a picnic table in Douthat State Park among the trees and nature when he disclosed the news.

Swallowing her bite of sandwich, Becky could not believe what she heard. "Are you sure?"

"Of course I'm sure."

"When did she take it?"

"This morning."

"Where'd she take it?"

"Hell, I don't know!" Exasperated, he got up and began to pace. "What are we going to do? How are we going to keep track of the money now?"

Becky knew she was in charge of this situation, but she thought she could count on Billy to keep his cool. "Look. You need to go back to the bank and just stay cool. Don't say anything to anyone and don't act nervous."

"But what do I do if she comes back to the bank?" Billy continued to pace. "What do I do if the cops show up?"

Becky laughed. "She's not calling no cops. Why would she?"

Billy turned and looked at her. "How do you know?"

"Think moron," Becky stood. "They don't know where the money came from either. They've been asking around and doing research about a bank robbery back in the sixties."

"So?"

"So, if this is stolen money the cops might be able to trace it. I don't know because it's been so long, but maybe." The look on Billy's face was a reaction she did not expect. Fear filled his eyes as he began to rock side to side and he looked down at the ground. "What have you done?" In her heart she knew. "You've spent some of the money!"

"No. No. I haven't," he lied, turning his back to her.

"Yes, you have!" She could not believe what she already knew. "Have you lost your mind?" Rising from the picnic bench and walking around him she grabbed Billy by the tie. Pulling him close to her she explained to him in no uncertain terms that if she went to jail because of his ignorance he would pay. "Do I make myself clear?" He nodded. Releasing his tie, she shoved him backwards causing him to fall to the ground. "Where did you spend the money?"

Rising to his feet and brushing the dirt from the seat of his pants and elbows, he turned away as pain shot through his arm. "You've ruined my suit," he winced, holding his elbow with his hand. Billy dared not share that his elbow may be broken...not with Becky. *That knowledge would bring her too much joy.*

"Answer me!" She demanded. Silence answered her demand. Exasperated, she returned to the picnic table and packed up the remains of her lunch. Turning back to Billy, "I swear to you, if I go to jail because of your greed and ignorance, you will truly regret anything you did to jeopardize my freedom." Heading back toward town, Becky knew she had messed up royally bringing Billy in on the deal.

~20~

With the money secured in the new safe deposit box, Susan headed toward Clifton Forge. Taking route two twenty, she enjoyed the drive after escaping the traffic of downtown Roanoke. The pastures spread as far as the eyes could see to the west with mountains lining the east. The well maintained roadway stretched like a black ribbon between the Virginia green. Passing through small hamlets sprinkled along the ribbon she reached the tiny hamlet of Iron Gate. Very soon she would need to decide whether to go to the cabin or the inn. She chose the cabin. *Even if no progress has been made on the construction today, at least I can sit by the river and clear my mind.*

Heading east toward the interstate, Susan thought she passed Becky in Cliftondale Park headed westbound. Waving, her wave was not returned. *Uhm. I guess she didn't see me.* Dialing Becky's number, the voice that answered sounded irritated.

"Hello."

"Becky, Susan."

"Oh. Hey." Susan's phone practically froze from Becky's response.

Ignoring the chill, she continued. "Hey, I think we just passed in Cliftondale Park." Susan tried to not sound put off.

Not wanting to confirm her location, Becky asked what Susan wanted.

"Would you like to have dinner this evening? I know we've talked about getting together. Thought maybe if you were available this evening we could get together?"

With other things on her mind, the last thing Becky wanted to do was have dinner with Susan. She needed to get to Richmond to start her research. "Look. I'd love to, but I'm heading out of town."

"Oh really?" This disclosure surprised Susan. "You looked like you were heading in town."

"I'm leaving shortly." Irritation was evident in her tone.

"Oh. Ok. Well, we'll get together when you get back." Dead air answered her. Looking at her phone she realized the call had been disconnected. *Uhm. Well, maybe nature did it.* Giving Becky the benefit of the doubt, Susan laid her phone on the car seat as she exited the interstate onto route forty-two.

Disconnecting the call from Susan, Becky instantly dialed another number. The male voice answered with just a "hello."

"The problem we expected has come to fruition. Evidently Mr. Clark has dipped into the funds that had been deposited in the box." Becky's disclosure was met with silence. "The funds need to be located and retrieved and the problem needs to be eliminated." Again, the disclosure was met with silence. Becky then disconnected the call. The voice on the other end removed the battery from his phone and smashed the phone with his boot. He would dispose of it in Lake Moomaw after he eliminated the problem.

~21~

The steel beams had been placed atop the pylons forming a sort of tic-tac-toe board. Nothing else had been completed. *Well, that's something I guess.* Grabbing a lawn chair she had left beside of one of the pylons, Susan made her way to the river.

The mountain bordered the river on the other side causing the water to escape up the bank toward her house when the heavy rains fell in the mountains west of there. The rocks further west of the house created rapids when the water was high, which it was today. Wading into the cold water, it reached up to her knees. Looking up river, she kept her eyes open for any snakes floating down. Her eyes also scanned the side of the mountain looking for any inhabitants that may be showing an interest in her. She saw none.

Moving back to the shore as her legs began to numb from the cold, she sat in her chair allowing her mind to drift away. *It is going to be so nice to be able to do this every day.* Her mind then turned to the money. *I wish Dewey was here. I need to go to the State Library to read newspapers.* Her thoughts were interrupted by her phone.

Dewey's voice came through the speaker. "Is the money stashed in the new box?"

"Hello to you," Susan answered. "You know it is."

"Ok. So, what are you going to do now?"

"I'm going to Richmond," she responded matter-of-factly. "You wanna join me?"

"When you going?"

Sighing, "I think I'll go tonight so I can be there when they open in the morning."

"Well, I can be there around noon. I'll meet you at the library." Disconnecting the call, Dewey notified his boss he would be taking a few more days off.

~22~

The drive to Richmond was uneventful. Becky decided to stay at the Hilton on Broad Street downtown. Located just three blocks from the State Library, she could park in their deck and walk. *It would probably be nice to get out and walk after spending all day sitting.* The drive into town was challenging with rush hour. She decided to check into the hotel first. Looking at the time, she realized the library would close in fifteen minutes. *I guess I'll have to wait until tomorrow to start my research.*

Looking through the tourist information on the desk, Becky quickly realized that all of the food establishments appeared to be located in the direction of Cary Street. *Well, I'll get my walk after all.* Exiting the hotel, she turned east to walk three blocks to the Capital Ale House. It felt good to stretch her legs, but the cacophony of traffic noises and horns blaring assaulted her ears. *Geez! Who in the world would want to live in all this noise?* Entering the Ale House she claimed a table for two. The noise was blocked out as the door closed and soft soothing music emanated from the speakers.

~23~

Night had fallen long before Susan arrived in the River City. She had spent time here before and enjoyed the vibe of the Fan District. This trip would be completely consumed with unearthing any information she could find in the library about the robbery. *It will be good to have Dewey helping. We can read twice as many newspapers.*

Checking into the Marriott on Broad Street downtown, she noticed they had built a Hilton right across the street. *Hum. Business must be booming in Richmond to warrant two five star hotels directly across the street from each other.* With the night getting late, she decided to order room service. Doing so allowed her to slip out of her street clothes and slip on her sweats and t-shirt; she then texted Dewey her room number.

Opening her laptop, she decided to, once again, access the library website as she waited on her food. Noting the various microfilms that contained the copies of the Daily Review she was interested in, it appeared there were four rolls that covered the time period. *This is going to take some time.*

The knock on the door announced the arrival of her dinner. Opening the door, she was greeted by Dewey. "What are you doing here? Pulling her brother into the room she gave him a huge hug. "I didn't think you were coming until tomorrow."

"Thought I'd get here tonight so we could get started early in the morning. Do you have a place for me to lay my head?" He looked around the room to see two queen sized beds.

"I believe I may," Susan laughed as another knock came from the door. "That must be dinner."

Opening the door, the busboy pushed the cart into the room. It contained a bottle of wine and two dinners. "But, I only ordered one," Susan declared.

Dewey laughed. "I called in just after you and ordered room service knowing I would be there shortly. When they told me they had just received an order for that room, I instructed them to deliver them at the same time."

Handing the busboy a tip, she closed the door. "Well, I got the Caesar salad. What did you get?" Uncovering the second meal, she revealed a filet mignon with sautéed vegetables and baked potato. "Mmmm. Good thing I ordered a red." She smiled. "Well, I hope you are paying for this and it's not on my room tab."

"Let's eat." Grabbing the wine bottle, Dewey opened it and poured some in each glass. Handing a glass to Susan, he clicked the two together. "To success."

Susan smiled. "To success."

~24~

As the sun sank behind the mountains Gary headed toward Potts Creek and the home of Billy Clark. A long red brick ranch home sitting at the edge of civilization; it was the last house before heading over the mountain to West Virginia. The property backed up to the mountain looming over the land. The creek the area drew its name from ran between the two. No street lights illuminated the night allowing him to secret himself just across the street in a grove of trees. Parking his vehicle just down the roadway at the convenience store, Gary had hiked west just a half a mile to find the grove where he now waited.

The night grew darker as the sun completely disappeared behind the mountain. He could hear the night creatures coming to life. He hoped the bears and other creatures would not come down off the mountain until he had finished his mission. The one thing he and Becky could not afford was a weak link. Before eliminating the link, he would need to find out what happened to the money. *If any was out there in circulation, it was just a matter of time before it would be called into question and the FBI alerted. After all, when was the last time money from the nineteen fifties in really good condition was in circulation?*

Checking the time, the hour approached nine. *This guy needs to get home.* Just then, lights approached from town. Slowing as the car approached, it turned in and pulled down the long driveway coming to a stop beside the house. A spotlight illuminated the yard allowing the occupant to see his way to the house.

Gary approached on foot after giving Billy time to enter his home. Knocking on the backdoor, he waited. "Who is it?"

"It's Gary." He responded.

"Hey Gary. Come on in." Billy stood back allowing Gary to enter. "What are you doing out here?"

Entering the sparsely furnished family room, Gary hesitated. "Uh, we need to talk." Looking around, he noticed there was only a rocking chair, a mission style chair and a TV precariously perched on a nineteen sixties TV tray. The curtains were your latest towel selection at the dollar store in a lovely shade of chocolate brown.

Sitting in the attached kitchen was a sad looking bistro set with a single chair. Chipped tile covered the kitchen floor and extended into the family room.

"Sure, sure. What's up?" Closing the door to keep out the night air, Billy motioned for Gary to have a seat.

"Nah man. I'm good." Suddenly, Gary felt nervous. He had never killed anyone before and really wasn't up to killing Billy. He would be satisfied just finding out where the money was and convincing Billy to keep his mouth shut. Looking down at the nineteen seventies tile, Gary mustered the nerve to do what he needed to do. "Look man. Becky knows you took the money and she wants it back. Now!"

Turning away from Gary, Billy walked to the sink retrieving a glass and filling it with water from the faucet. With his back turned, he responded. "What money? I don't have any money." Looking out the kitchen window at the darkness, he knew he was less than convincing.

Gary had followed him into the kitchen. "Then where is it?"

"I don't know what you're talking about."

Growing frustrated with the evasiveness, Gary walked toward the stove. Sitting to the right of it was a knife block filled with a variety of kitchen knives. Retrieving the knife with the largest handle, he knew it would be supporting the largest blade. "Look man," as he turned to face Billy. Just then, lights illuminated the front windows signaling that Billy had more company. Gary tensed even more than before. The crunch of the driveway gravel stopped, followed by a knock on the backdoor.

Moving to the door, Billy opened it to find Cliff standing there. "Cliff! Come in. Come in," standing back to allow his entrance. Temporary relief flooded through Billy as Cliff stepped through the door and Billy motioned to draw Cliff's attention toward Gary."

Caught by surprise, Cliff stopped. "Oh. I thought you were alone."

Puzzled, Billy looked at Gary. "Why would you think that?"

"Because there are no cars in the drive but yours."

Hearing that declaration, Billy looked at Gary. It was then he realized Gary was not there to just talk.

"Yeah." Gary returned the knife to the block taking care to draw his hand over the wood to smear whatever fingerprints he may have left. "Uh, my truck died down at the convenience store. I walked up here to get Billy to give me a ride back home."

"Oh. Well, I can give you a ride." Cliff turned to Billy. "Look, I know it's late, but I've been tied up at a job all day. Is there any news on my loan?"

"Uh, yeah. Yeah. It was approved today." What little color Billy had seemed to have drained from his already pallid face. "Uh, you can come by tomorrow afternoon and sign the papers. We can transfer the money to your account as soon as you do."

"Well, that's great news. Look. I gotta get going." Moving to leave, he stopped at the door. "Gary. You wanna ride?"

Knowing that the mission needed to be scrubbed, Gary accepted the offer, leaving his truck sitting at the convenience store. *I'll get it tomorrow.*

The ride back home was quiet. Thanking Cliff as he exited the truck, Gary went into his house and grabbed a beer. Sitting in the dim light of the lone lamp in the living room he knew that if Billy turned up dead tonight, he could be a suspect. Finishing his beer, he retrieved another and returned to his chair.

~25~

The din of the morning traffic noise was muffled by the thick glass window of the hotel room. Pulling the curtains back, Susan gazed down on the traffic as Dewey showered. On the sidewalk below, the men were accompanied by women dressed the same; black or navy blue suits. Each carrying either a smart slim briefcase or a backpack slung over one shoulder as they made their way to their respective offices. *Oh, I used to be in that life. I used to enjoy it, but no more. I need to make my own way now. No more nine to five for me.*

"Watching the worker bees?" Susan turned to see her brother wearing only a towel wrapped around his waist and water dripping from his head. "Your turn."

"Thanks." Susan headed for the bath.

Across the roadway, the same din assaulted the window occupied by Becky. She too peered out upon the masses moving toward their offices. Waiting for nine o'clock she knew the library would open and she would be able to learn who robbed the bank and when. She could feel her anticipation growing.

Jarred from her thoughts, her cell phone announced an incoming call. Looking at the screen she knew it was Gary.

Bracing herself, she touched the screen to connect the call and then again to activate the speaker. "Hi Gary. All done?"

He hesitated. "Not quite."

"What do you mean, "Not quite? Irritation replaced her anticipation. "I thought you were going to take care of it last night."

"I was," he confirmed. "I went to visit him last night."

Her irritation grew. "And?"

"And we were interrupted."

Listening to his explanation she could not believe his luck. *What are the chances of Cliff stopping in at the same time Gary is there?* "So, what are you going to do about it?"

"Well, first I'm going to retrieve my truck."

Becky was not amused. "After that."

Hesitating before he delivered the news, "We need to wait. Give it some time. I couldn't go back last night because I'd be a suspect. So, I'm going to wait a few days and try again."

Frustration filled her. "We can't wait too long. We need to know what he did with the money."

Agreeing, Gary assured her that everything would be fine and they would retrieve the money. "Look. You just get the research done and I'll take care of Billy. I'll see you when you get back."

Disconnecting the call, Becky returned to the window to see someone resembling Susan walking along Broad Street Road with a man a few inches taller than her. Looking at the clock she realized it was now nine o'clock. Grabbing her bag she headed for the library.

~26~

The gray granite steps led to floor-to-ceiling glass doors opening into an atrium. Walking through a second set of matching glass doors, Susan and Dewey entered the expansive first floor of the library. Stopping just inside they were mesmerized by the grandeur. Gray granite walls rose on either side to the second floor which was walled by glass exposing many of the wooden bookcases holding hundreds of books. Light oak wood panels interrupted the granite to frame assorted displays of coming exhibits and available resources. The grand staircase, directly in front of them beyond the security checkpoint, directed the eye upward to a landing. Just beyond, there was more light-wood paneling topped with more glass.

"Whoa!" Dewey breathed as his eyes followed the staircase to the top landing. Susan just stood there speechless.

"Can I help you?" Snapping back to reality, they moved toward the checkpoint. "Place your bags on the counter and empty your pockets of anything metal. Please walk through the metal detector," directed the security guard.

Clearing security, they made their way to the circulation desk located behind the partial glass wall at the top of the stairs. "Hello," Susan began. "We're here to look at some old newspapers."

Looking up from her computer screen, the Archivist smiled. "Do you have a library card?"

Susan explained she had applied for one on line, but her brother did not have one. After receiving their cards they were directed to the left and told someone in the research room would be able to help them locate their materials.

Thirty minutes later they had received instructions on how to use the microfilm machines located at the back of the library next to the glass walls looking down on the grand staircase. The librarian showed them where to retrieve the rolls corresponding with the dates of the Daily Review they were interested in. Having previously researched the library records, Susan knew there were four rolls. Retrieving all four, they began their research.

~27~

Impressed by the grand staircase, Becky stopped at the top so she could turn around and absorb the beauty of the workmanship. The gray granite glistened in the sunlight that came through the skylights. Turning three hundred and sixty degrees, Becky stopped facing the window across the expanse of air that separated her from the microfilm machines. Susan and Dewey were intently staring at the machines as if spellbound. *So it was Susan I saw.*

Hesitating, she wasn't sure if she should leave or stay. *If I leave, that delays my research. But if I stay I'll run into them and they'll know I'm researching the bank robbery.* Taking a step up, she hesitated and took a step back down. She stopped and looked at Susan. Just then Susan looked her straight in her eyes. Wishing to vanish right where she stood, Becky was still unsure what to do. Susan waved.

Knowing she was busted, Becky finished mounting the stairs to the circulation desk. "Hello, can you tell me how to get to the microfilm machines?" The librarian directed her into the research room. Taking her time, Becky needed to come up with a cover story quick. "Hi Susan. Dewey."

"Becky. What are you doing here?"

Taking the empty chair beside Dewey, she glanced at the monitor. "What are ya'll doing here?" There was a copy of a newspaper looking back at her. With the print so small, she was unable to read it without focusing intently.

Dewey responded. "Oh, just some genealogy. Why are you here?" An awkward silence filled the distance between them. Each knew that the truth would not be spoken between them in this situation. Some how they all knew they were looking for the same information, but each was unwilling to share.

Hesitating before answering, Becky finally responded. "Uh, I'm uh, researching some land in Bath County I'm thinking about buying. I need to get a topo map. Well, I'll leave you to your research. I need to head home in a bit." Rising Becky returned to the circulation desk to inquire about copies of the Daily Review. In her heart she knew she would be unsuccessful as long as they were in the library. She inquired anyway, with no luck. After obtaining a library card, she was directed to the map room. *Gotta at least make it look good.*

By noon, Becky had descended the grand staircase while Susan and Dewey stared at their monitors. Making her way back to her hotel room, she needed to decide if she should stay or return to the mountains to research another day. *What to do, what to do.*

~28~

Placing his forefinger on the screen, Dewey turned to Susan, "Look at this." Susan rolled her chair closer to Dewey's. Reading the screen; MOUNTAIN BANK ROBBED BY 3.

"Wow!" She continued to read. Dewey read also adjusting the screen to help them finish the article. "Ok. So, the bank WAS robbed." Susan pushed her chair back which allowed her to cross her legs. Dewey interpreted it as a defensive move.

"They didn't name any suspects." Confirming what they had read.

"Print it out so we can take it with us. What's the date of that paper?" Susan responded. The two continued to read in unison, finishing the one article and moving to the next edition. There was nothing there. They continued to scan through papers finally finding the next article; 100k STOLEN FROM MOUNTAIN BANK.

"Well, here ya go!" Dewey proclaimed. "One hundred k was stolen."

"Yes, but we had a hundred and fifty k." Susan pointed out. "Where did the other fifty k come from?"

Stopping and turning to face Susan, "Gosh, I don't know. Maybe they didn't disclose the entire amount taken?"

"In a small town like Clifton Forge, everyone knows everything. If it was more than a hundred thousand, they would have said the amount. Let's keep looking." Susan turned back to her monitor containing the reel she had been perusing. Nothing was reported in any of the papers she read. Dewey found several more articles on his reels but nothing to indicate any arrests or any additional information about the amount of money that had been taken. Neither found any other articles about any robberies that would include the significant amount of fifty thousand dollars.

Hitting the rewind button on the last reel, Dewey observed they knew everything they needed to know about the happenings in their little town about the time of the bank robbery. "I doubt the Covington paper would have any more information."

"Well, I think we need to go through it just to be safe." Dewey looked at her like she had lost her mind. "We're already here. Why not? Let me have the reels and I'll order the ones for the "Covington Virginian."

"Wait, I'm tired. It's late. Why don't we call it a day and come back tomorrow."

Research the next day revealed no new information, but they did see Becky ascending the stairway. "Didn't she say she was going home yesterday?" Susan was perplexed.

Confirming Susan's observation, he added, "Maybe she found something about the property she didn't like and needs to reconfirm?" Susan's facial expression clearly said she didn't buy it one minute.

~29~

The light in the family room didn't illuminate when Billy clicked the switch on. "Damn." Not thinking it was odd the outside spotlight didn't illuminate when he pulled into the drive, he just assumed the bulb was burnt out and decided to take care of the problem over the week-end. *It's too dark to climb a ladder tonight and I don't have time during the day. I'll just have to come home in the dark the rest of the week.* Moving toward the kitchen light switch, it did not illuminate the overhead light either. *There was no storm today. Why is the power out?*

Digging in the drawer beside the kitchen sink, he found the flashlight that was many lumens brighter than his phone light. The D-cell kel-light was cold in his hand. It was large enough to give a comfortable hand grip and long enough to secure it under his armpit when flipping switches in the breaker box. Opening the basement door, it released the cold air below the house sending a chill up his spine.

Descending into the darkness, each step gave its own little squeak of recognition to his footstep. *I hate this basement. Always have. I really hate it in the dark.* The beam of light shone across the stairway helping him make his way to the basement floor. Stopping midway down Billy thought he heard something move. *Oh dear God, please don't be a raccoon or skunk.*

Remembering his confrontation in the basement with a raccoon during his youth brought fear to mind.

At the delicate age of fourteen, he had made his way to the basement to address the blown breaker controlling his bedroom electronics. Unbeknownst to him, a raccoon had found its way through a screen door that had been left ajar earlier in the evening. As he walked across the basement, the raccoon felt threatened and chased him up the stairs stopping only because Billy had managed to slam the door closed before it could scurry in behind him. Screaming like a school girl, terror filled his being. He'll never forget the roar of laughter from his father and the words that followed; "sissy", "little girl" and more.

His father walked to the bedroom to retrieve his shotgun. Once the racket on the other side of the basement door stopped, he opened it. Clearly, the raccoon had given up and gone back to its lair in the basement. "Where were you when it came at you?" His father demanded.

"Over by the washing machine."

"Stay here." As the basement door closed, Billy could hear his father's heavy construction boots clomping down the stairs. Silence. Billy waited. Then suddenly a blast from the gun caused him and his mother to jump. They heard his father call out a profanity and then discharged another round followed by a cheer and laugh. "Got it!"

Billy then heard his father's work books climbing the steps. As the door opened the now deceased raccoon was thrust through the opening as his father followed. Clomping toward the backdoor, his father disappeared into the darkness to dispose of the now deceased critter. Billy shook as he remembered that night.

Continuing to make his way down the dark stairs, he held his breath willing his ears to hear supernaturally. Stepping onto the concrete floor he turned toward where he knew the breaker box to be.

"Hello Billy." The disembodied voice came from the darkness.

Turning in the direction of the voice, he shone the light in the face of the friend who had visited a couple nights before. "Gary! Man, what are you doing down here?"

"Get the light out of my eyes." Prepared for such a reaction, Gary had worn sunglasses to avoid being blinded by any lights shone in his eyes. As ordered, the light was extinguished and they were plunged into a darkness blacker than black. Waiting a minute in silence, Gary then illuminated a pen light that gave minimum illumination to the surroundings.

Shining the light into Billy's eyes, he began the inquisition. "Where's the money, Billy?" He waited. No response. Again, "Billy, where's the money?"

Looking down to avoid the light, he responded, "What money?"

"You know what money."

"No, I don't," he insisted.

Allowing a long sigh to escape from him, Gary continued. "The money you took from the safe deposit box." He waited, but no response was forthcoming. "Look man, you know we know you took the money. It would be best if you just tell me what you did with it so I can recover it." He again waited.

Continuing to look down, Billy insisted he had no idea what Gary was talking about. Continuing to plead his innocence he insisted that if he had taken any money his house would not look like it did. Going on to explain he would have bought furniture and fixed the exterior of the home that needed repair, he continued to insist he took no money from any safe deposit box.

Growing tired of the game, Gary felt it now necessary to motivate Billy. Taking several steps toward him, he grabbed Billy by the arm and spun him around. "Get down on your knees."

"What?"

"You heard me," insisted Gary. "Get down on your knees." Reluctantly, Billy obeyed. "Put your hands behind your back?"

Fear filled Billy. "What are you going to do?" The basement had always been his scary space. Now, that fear was becoming reality at the hands of someone he believed to be a friend.

Putting the pen light between his teeth, Gary retrieved the zip ties from his back pocket, securing Billy's hands. "Now, I don't want to do this, but you must tell me where the money is."

As the night wore on, Gary made no progress. Billy continued to insist that he had no knowledge of the money and had not taken any.

Not having the desire to hurt his old friend, Gary walked to the breaker box and threw the main breaker. Suddenly, the basement was illuminated along with the exterior lights. Cutting the zip tie loose, Gary commanded, "Get up. Look man, I'm really sorry about all this. I believe you. I don't think you know about the money." With that, Gary left through the back basement door disappearing into the night.

Billy rose from his knees and ascended the stairs back to his family room. Punching a number into his cell phone he waited for an answer. "They are worried about the money." He listened. "I think I convinced him I didn't know anything about the money. Time will tell."

"Are you sure it's well hidden?" The stranger on the other end was not pleased with the news.

"They will never find it." Billy declared. "No one will." Billy listened and then disconnected the call. Grabbing a beer from the fridge, he sat down to catch his favorite show. He chuckled to himself. *Yep, they're sweating.*

The old man disconnected on his end as well as he took a sip from his scotch and viewed the sleepy little town from the picture window of his home at the top of Jefferson Avenue. Having been the manager of Mountain National Bank at the time of the robbery, he was supposed to have received a cut from the proceeds for his inside part of the robbery. He knew it was against bank policy to have the vault unlocked during the day. Policy dictated tellers would get their draws at the beginning of their shift and then the vault gate would be locked until just before closing. Two people were needed to unlock the gate to allow the tellers to return their drawers at closing, but Billy's grand-uncle had chosen to help his buddies…in exchange for a cut of the proceeds.

There had been no indication he would be double crossed. Nicely was to take the money and hide it until the heat of the investigation cooled. Then, the four of them would get together and divvy up the take. But that never happened.

Muncy never returned for his cut and Fitzgerald was killed in a crash. Nicely had said the whereabouts of the money died with Fitzgerald. *I knew he was lying to me back then.* Taking another sip of his scotch, he knew the money was within his grasp. He just needed to find the remaining hundred and forty thousand. *Hell, Billy can keep the ten grand. He earned it keeping me informed about large deposits and checking safe deposit boxes.* Pouring another glass of scotch, he knew time was of the essence for him to be reunited with the missing money.

~30~

The separate vehicles had prevented them from discussing what they had learned at the library. There was only one hundred k taken from the bank and no other major robberies in the area before or after; at least in a reasonable time period around it. Topping North Mountain, Susan called Dewey who followed, suggesting they stop by the cabin. Agreeing, he said he would run down to the market and get some beer.

Great progress had been made in the three days they had been gone; the floor and four exterior walls were up and they were working on interior walls. "Hey Cliff! Ya'll are coming along."

Looking down from one of the bedroom windows, Cliff agreed. "We'll be under roof in a couple days."

"That's great! Can I come up?"

"Sure. The river side porch is stable enough for you to climb up on. Come on up and take a look around. It looks much better than the last time you saw the inside of your home." He laughed thinking about all the walls she had demolished before he could get to it.

Balancing up the steps to the soon to be back porch, Susan entered the cavernous room not yet delineated by interior walls. The chalk marks on the sub-flooring showed the framers where to put the various walls. "So, let me see if I can figure this out." Moving through the house she named the various rooms, looking at Cliff for confirmation. Excitement filled her as she visualized her new home. "So, the roof goes on in a couple days?"

"Yep. Then the plumbers, HVAC and electricians will come in and do their thing."

"So, are ya'll ahead of schedule?"

Cliff shook his head. "Nope. Right on. I need you to go to Roanoke and pick out the fixtures, flooring and cabinets. I'll be bringing by paint samples for you to choose the colors too."

Smiling, Susan expressed her excitement just as Dewey appeared at the porch door. "Beer anyone?" He grinned.

"Not for me. I'm working."

Susan took the offered beer. "Here, let me give you the nickel tour." Ten minutes later they were walking toward the river sipping on their beers.

"The house is going to be awesome, Mutt," Dewey laughed. She punched his shoulder.

The discussion turned to the money and what they had found. It was agreed that the hundred thousand came from the bank, but how did it end up in the walls of their childhood home? Neither could imagine their father robbing a bank. He was a farmer. He helped the needy. He occasionally did odd jobs around town but bank robber?

They just could not imagine. The fifty thousand was still a mystery. They checked all of the papers from Covington and Clifton Forge for the time period and no articles indicated any other robberies in the area. Nor were there any articles about any arrests of the three people who robbed the bank. "In such a small town, there is no way no one knew who did the robbery," Susan observed. "Someone knows."

Dewey agreed. "My question is, what was Becky doing at the library? Don't you find it odd she showed up while we were there?" Susan agreed. "Do you think she was following us?"

"Why would she? She doesn't know anything about the money." Susan hesitated. "Unless Billy told her."

"Well, this is definitely a mystery. We both need to watch our backs and play it close to the vest. Don't tell anyone about the money."

Nodding her head, "Who'd a thought this sleepy little down had such secrets? I'm going to head back into town. You coming?" She started toward the cars.

"Nah. I'm going to head home. I need to show up for work so I don't get fired."

Susan laughed. "Yeah, at least until we find out about the money."

~31~

"Has anyone seen Mr. Clark?" Angie, the junior teller needed a signature for a cashiers' check and she believed Billy Clark to be the only one who could sign.

"He went out for a meeting around noon," Marie shared. "He said he was going to get a bite to eat and be back around two. You need something?"

Hesitating, "I need his signature for this cashiers' check."

"Here, I'll sign for him." Moving toward Angie, Marie glanced out the large floor to ceiling windows to see a marked police car driving down the alley between Farrar's Drug Store and the community center. Not thinking anything of it, she signed the check and returned to her window.

Two o'clock came and went without Billy returning to the bank. Both Angie and Marie found this odd for someone as punctual as Billy. "Are you sure he didn't take the afternoon off?" Angie was getting a little worried. "It's not like him to leave work without saying something to someone."

"I'll call his cell." Marie was worried as well but didn't want to appear so. Dialing his number the call was answered by his voicemail. Disconnecting, she then called his house number. That too was answered by a machine. Knowing his parents were deceased, she decided to call the hospital. *Maybe he had a medical emergency while at lunch.*

"Any luck?" Angie was counting her drawer preparing to close her window for the night. With only ten minutes before closing she knew there would be no additional customers. Six o'clock brought people into their homes to enjoy dinner with their families. The strangers in town had no need for the banks services with everyone using credit cards now.

"No. Nothing." Marie could not conceal her concern. Billy was the epitome of punctuality and an excellent employee. He ran the branch by the book and never deviated from the policies or procedures.

Carrying her drawer to the vault, Angie turned toward Marie. "Should we call the police? Something has definitely happened to him. This is completely out of character for him."

Marie nodded. "Yes, this is. I'll call it in."

With the report made, there was little more Angie and Marie could do but wait. Billy's vehicle still sat in his parking spot on Main Street. The same place he parked everyday. Allowing her hand to run along the fender as she walked past, Marie said a little prayer. Reaching the corner of Commercial and Main, the girls said their goodbyes. Angie headed toward the tavern. Marie walked toward McCormick Street and her home. She always took advantage of these warm days to save on gas and get a little exercise.

~32~

The body lay below Ridgeway Street along side the trickling Smith Creek as cars and trucks traveled above. Black and blue bruises covered the face as if he had taken a significant beating before he was put out of his misery. His shirttail was out of the waistband of his navy blue dress pants with scuffed knees. Dirt clung to the wet lower third of the pants and the lone black leather penny loafer. The blue argyle sock on the right foot was drenched and dirty since it was missing the loafer twin. Clearly, he had spent some time in the creek before his demise.

The gash to the back of his head matched the ridge of the large boulder beside the creek. Blood smeared down the side of the boulder to the back of Billy's head. His eyes gave a vacant stare into the distance looking up to the underside of the bridge the citizens called Ridgeway Street. Hidden by the bridge piles, it could be days until he is found, unless someone knows where to look.

The patrol car passed by, not noticing anything unusual. Kids skipping school would sometimes hang out under Ridgeway Street attempting to avoid classes, parents and anyone else curious as to why they weren't in school. The local homeless would sometimes bed down under the bridge at night or drink there during the day. Those circumstances were the officer's focus; not the search for a missing bank official.

Not seeing anything out of the ordinary, the officer continued to travel behind the assorted businesses that called Ridgeway Street home. Many of the buildings reached the ground two stories below the pavement of the main roadway. Others sat on pylons that lifted them up to meet the pavement. As night fell, he knew the businesses would be closing for the night and the town would be going to sleep…for the most part.

Tourists would be moving about the sidewalks visiting the various restaurants and tonight's concert at the Masonic Theatre. None would be coming down behind the businesses. There was no reason for them to.

Taking a seat at the bar, Angie ordered her usual beverage. "Hi Martha. Have you seen Billy Clark today?"

"Not today, Angie." sliding her wine in front of her. "What would you like to eat?"

Knowing he had other places to eat, Martha's response didn't fill Angie with concern. *I'll just have to check the other eateries.* "Uh, just let me have a French dip with fries and cole slaw. Thanks."

With dinner finished, Angie made her way to the other eateries in town. No one had seen Billy all day. *Where could he be? It is so unlike him to disappear like this.* Concerned, but with nothing to go on, she decided to head home. Returning to her car, she saw that Billy's was still parked in his spot.

Saying a little prayer for him, she drove off, heading over Ridgeway to Low Moor.

~33~

Several days had passed since Billy had disappeared. Talk around town was that he had absconded with funds from a variety of bank deposit boxes and left town. Because of this, bank examiners and the FBI had descended upon the little, not so sleepy town and began their investigation. Contacting everyone who leased a safe deposit box, the investigators requested the lessees come down to review the contents of their respective boxes to determine if anything was missing. They had each been given an appointed time. Susan's was four o'clock Friday afternoon.

Pacing back and forth along the river, Susan worried into her phone. "Dewey, how am I going to explain renting an empty box?"

"You don't need to explain anything." Dewey assured her. "Just tell them nothing is missing. I doubt they will go in the room with you."

"Are you sure?" Susan took a sip of her beer trying to calm her nerves.

"Yes. Just tell them nothing is missing and leave it at that."

"OK. When are you coming in town?"

Hesitating, Dewey couldn't keep running to his sister every time she had an issue. "I'll be in next week-end." Attempting to change the subject, "How's the construction going?"

"It's going. It's under roof."

"Great. OK. I'll see you next week." Disconnecting the call, he knew his sister would be fine. She always panicked when initially confronted by a dilemma, but she also performed well under pressure.

~34~

As four o'clock approached, Susan headed into the bank. It appeared to be business as usual except for the several suits behind the desks and teller stations. Greeted by a tall dark haired gentleman dressed in a Brooks Brothers suit, Susan informed him she had a four o'clock appointment to look in her safe deposit box. Identifying himself as Agent Delano with the FBI he directed her toward a woman standing by the entrance to the vault. She did not smile as Susan approached, only spoke. "Your name ma'am?" Maintaining a businesslike decorum, she looked at Susan and then down at the clipboard on the counter beside her.

"Uh, Susan. Susan Nicely."

Making a check mark beside Susan's name, she looked up. "Right this way."

Following the woman into the vault, Susan produced her key to her box as the woman inserted hers into one of the locks. Handing her key to the woman, the box vault door was unlocked and the box was slid from its singular vault.

Fifteen minutes later, Susan stepped out onto Ridgeway Street headed toward the tavern. Hoping Cliff would show up, she needed a friend to talk with, to have a beer with.

The scream reverberated off of the bricks of Farrar's Drug Store causing it to travel across Ridgeway Street and bounced off the bricks of the bank. Followed by a second scream and then a third, chills ran down Susan's spine. Spinning in the direction of the sound, she saw several teenagers spilling from the mouth of the alley, some losing whatever they had previously eaten others collapsing to the sidewalk. "Call the police!" A voice screamed.

Susan ran across the road reaching one of the teenage girls sobbing on the sidewalk. "What happened?" The sobbing girl could not respond. The agent standing at the door of the bank had also heard the screams and ran to the teens. The boys shared there was a body under the roadway and "it is really gross". Looking at Susan, she could tell that what the teens said made no sense to the agent.

"This roadway is a bridge. Go down that alley and you'll see what the kids are talking about."

Following Susan's suggestion, Delano made his way down the alley. Coming to the bottom of the roadway he was surprised to find bridge structure supporting what he thought was a normal roadway. Surveying the area he observed a creek running along a rocky terrain. There were dirt patches separating several of the large boulders and there seemed to be an abundance of flies in the corner area of the supports. A putrid smell entered his nostrils causing him to put his nose in the crook of his arm. Moving deeper under the bridge the sight that greeted him almost made him throw up.

The body laid along side the creek with one sock foot in the water. The blonde matted head lay beside a large boulder with a brown smear trailing from the top to the decomposing head on the dirt. Maggots fed on what was supposed to be the mouth, eyes and nose. The shirttail was out of the waistband of the dress pants that were covered with the dirt surrounding the body. Clearly it had been there for a while.

Not needing to approach closer, Agent Delano turned to return to fresh air when he ran into the city police officer who had just pulled up. "Whatcha got?"

Moving as far away as he could from the source of the stench, Delano responded, "You got a dead male over there. Looks like he's been there a while. You're gonna need a forensics team."

"We don't have one." Embarrassment filled the officer's face. "I'll need to call the chief."

"Well, in the meantime you need to cordon off this area and don't let anyone in."

Becoming offended at being ordered by someone in a suit, the officer questioned, "Who are you?"

"Agent Delano, FBI. Do you have any other officers to help you?"

"We'll be calling in the State Police." Returning to the police unit, Officer Patterson retrieved the roll of police tape. Tying it to one of the piles of the bridge, he walked a wide perimeter ensuring no one could come close to the scene.

Delano returned to the top of the alley to find all of the teens sitting along the sidewalk. Two of the girls silently wept while the other two stared into the distance, unblinking. The boys stared at the sidewalk, not speaking. Agent Hanna, the woman who had escorted Susan into the vault, stood close by not speaking to any of the teens. Susan stood beside Agent Hanna, unable to speak after hearing the description of what the teens had found below where they stood.

The blue and gray state police unit turned off of Ridgeway into the alley. Slowly driving down the hill, he turned to park along side the town cruiser. Stepping out of his cruiser, the trooper advised the officer the forensics unit was enroute from Roanoke. They would be arriving within the hour. "In the meantime we need to separate and secure those kids sitting on the sidewalk and the crime scene."

"So, you taking over this investigation?" The officer was hoping he would respond affirmatively.

The trooper turned to face him. "Looks like since ya'll are shorthanded. I could use your help though until the forensics team shows up."

"Sure. Sure. Just let me advise dispatch to notify the chief I'll be tied up for a while. He might want to come down here anyway." Entering his cruiser, Officer Patterson keyed up his radio. Shortly after his communication to dispatch, the chief came walking around the back of Farrar's Drug Store.

"Chief? That was quick. Where's your car?" Patterson knew the chief occasionally conducted foot patrol but since it was so close to five o'clock he assumed he would be in his cruiser headed home.

"I was finishing up paperwork in the office. Dispatch gave me the heads up so I decided to walk over." Walking toward the police tape, he lifted the yellow psychological wall entering the crime scene.

"Chief!" Trooper Putnam called out. "You realize you've entered the crime scene?" The chief stopped. "You go any closer and you'll be tied up in court as a witness."

Stopping, Chief Craft turned to him. "Oh, I'm aware. We've had a missing banker. I just wanted to take a look at the body to see if it's him." He continued to move toward the body, crossing the creek. Approaching the body, he pulled out his cell phone and proceeded to take a photograph.

"What are you doing?" Trooper Putnam questioned.

Returning to the yellow wall, Chief Craft reminded the trooper that the crime scene was in his jurisdiction and that he was there at their request. As chief he was allowed to do as he pleased. "We are going to identify the body. Maybe the tellers can tell me what Billy Clark was wearing the last time they saw him."

Offended, the trooper could not believe what he was hearing. "Surely you aren't going to show these pictures to the tellers."

"Oh, no. No." The chief assured him. "That would be cruel and unusual punishment. Rest assured they will be fine." With that, the chief headed back to his office. "Let me know when you make positive ID."

Trooper Putnam found odd the statement that the tellers would be fine. *What is he up too? I need the Captain to get the Superintendent to call the Chief and let him know we are in charge.*

With the hands of the assorted time pieces around town moving past five, the sun dipped below the mountain ridge. Dusk fell over the town. The director of the community center allowed the agent and trooper to take possession of the center. The teens were moved inside as the curtains were pulled across the floor to ceiling windows facing the street, affording them the privacy required for the investigation. The parents had been notified and were arriving. Emotions ran high as the teens reunited with their parents. Sodas and pizzas were ordered and delivered in an effort to relax the teens and bring a sense of normalcy to the gathering, even though it was far from normal.

Trooper Putnam introduced himself to everyone and explained that each of the teens would be interviewed individually. He assured the parents that they would be present during all questioning. He also assured them that none of the teens were suspects; but witnesses. He went on to explain that counselors would be available for the students to talk with whenever they felt the need, at no cost to the parents. "Now, if we can begin, we hope to make this as quick and as painless as possible." With that, Patterson, Delano and Putnam, each invited a teen and their parents to join them in one of the three small meeting rooms at the back of the community center.

All of the questions were the same; why were they below Ridgeway? What time did they go down there; and what exactly did they see? As each interview concluded, the teens were allowed to go home with their parents. The students were told there may be additional questions.

~35~

The forensics team photographed the scene before illuminating the task lights making the area under the bridge as bright as high noon on a sunny day. The body had clearly been snacked on by whatever critters had moseyed by as well as flies, crickets and maggots. Lividity indicated the body had been in its current position for more than six hours. The blood had settled in the back of the body's legs and buttocks as well as the right side of the torso from the waist up into the head.

The presence of maggots indicated the body had been in decay for at least a week. The timeline was placing the corpse in the time period that the banker had disappeared. It was difficult to determine the corpse's identity due to the decay. That would be the job of the medical examiner if they could obtain any fingerprints from the remaining fingers or if there were any dental records available.

Finishing the job of processing the scene, the forensics techs allowed the medical techs to retrieve the body. Taking care to move the body, the state of decay was such that the body may drop pieces as it was moved. The black plastic body bag was zipped around the remains. It would contain any flesh or fluids that dropped from the body while being transported to the Medical Examiner's office in Roanoke.

~36~

Susan had left her name and phone number with the trooper who had taken control of the situation. She then made her way to the tavern where the talk was of the body discovered below Ridgeway. Rumors were that it was Billy Clark, the banker. This did not please Susan. If it was him, then the possibility of her recovering the ten thousand dollars he had stolen from her safe deposit box was very unlikely.

Entering the tavern, she saw that her favorite table was occupied by Cliff. Appearing to be alone she decided to join him. "Hi Cliff. Mind if I join you?"

Motioning toward the empty chair, he nodded. It was then that she saw he was on his phone. Feeling as if she was intruding, she signaled that she would be right back as she made her way to the bar. Ordering a double Jack on the rocks she asked the drink to be delivered to Cliff's table while she went to the restroom. Returning to Cliff's table she found he had finished his call. "Did you send me a double Jack?" He smiled.

She smiled. "No. I need it."

"Is it true there was a body under the bridge?"

Taking a deep sip of her Jack, "Yes. They say it may be Billy Clark."

Cliff could not believe what he was hearing. "How could that be?"

"I don't know. Did you get a call to come in and check your safe deposit box?" Susan drained her glass raising it to the bartender indicating another.

"I did. Slow down, Susan. You need to eat something."

Taking the menu from the table beside them, Susan perused the offerings. "You're right. If I don't I'll get drunk and I don't want that. I need to stay somewhat clearheaded."

Midnight approached as Susan made her way to the inn. Cliff had offered to give her a ride, but she convinced him she needed to walk it off. *Besides, it was a nice evening and this was a safe town. Or, at least it used to be. Hopefully it still is.* Leaving her car parked beside the bank she knew it would be best not to get behind the wheel. Falling on her bed, she was soon passed out.

~37~

Becky was greeted by a grainy black and white photo accompanied by the large headline "LOCAL BANKER MURDERED" when she opened her newspaper. Retrieving her glasses to get a better look at the photo, clearly it had been taken from a distance and cropped. Although the body appeared male the face was not identifiable so she had to assume it was Billy.

Three hours later Gary was waiting for her at the picnic table in Douthat State Park. Pulling her car into the parking spot she noticed him sitting on the table with his head hanging low toward his knees. "Did you get the money?" He didn't answer. "Gary, did you get the money?"

"No."

"Look at me." She commanded. "Why not?"

Staring at the bench of the picnic table where his feet rested, Gary didn't answer.

Exasperation filled her voice as it raised a couple of octaves. "Why not, Gary?"

Getting down from the table, Gary began to pace. "Look. I went to the house and Cliff showed up. I couldn't do anything with Cliff there."

"Did he stay all night?"

"No. But if anything had happened to Billy that night, I would have been a suspect."

"That was the first time you went," Becky pointed out. "What about the second time?"

Gary stopped and faced Becky. "Look, Billy said he didn't have the money. Why would he live like he was living if he had the money? Have you been in his house?" Gary waited. "Well?"

"I've not."

"Well, he has…or should I say, had, nothing. If he had the money, I believe he would have at least bought some damn curtains for the living room. He had TOWELS hanging at the window!"

Agreeing with his logic, Becky began to drill him for facts about the day Billy died. Gary's explanation seemed reasonable but there was no way to verify his whereabouts. "What if Cliff goes to the cops and tells them you were at Gary's house late?"

"It wasn't late. And besides, I had a good reason. My truck broke down at the convenience store, remember? Cliff gave me a ride home. Look. I didn't kill him and I didn't get the money."

"Well, where is it?"

"I don't know."

Realizing she was getting nowhere fast, Becky headed for her car. "Look. Find the money. We need to know if it was stolen during the robbery."

Perplexed, Gary followed Becky to her car. "How am I going to find that out?"

'I don't know. But you will." Closing her car door and starting the engine, Becky backed out and headed back into town. Waving through her sunroof she smiled leaving Gary standing in the dust with his hands on his hips. *What a wimp he is.* Jumping on the interstate, she headed home.

~38~

The newspaper lay open on the Louis IVX side table in one of the guest rooms of the red brick palatial estate topping McCormick Boulevard. The room not only offered a view of any traffic approaching up the hill, but also a view of the little town. The headline displayed just under the masthead did not please him. Neither did the photo. He felt it unnecessary and too gruesome for public consumption. He had come to town to recover the money that had disappeared so many years before only to learn it had been discovered. He had tried to cultivate the banker when he arrived in town to assist in locating the money. Billy's only job was to notify him if anyone made a significant deposit deemed reportable to the Feds. He would have been rewarded handsomely for his help if he had not helped himself to a small portion. Greed had led to his demise. Unfortunately, the visitor will never find out what happened to the missing ten thousand. *I guess I'll have to be happy with the hundred and forty thousand.* He needed to now find what happened to the remaining funds since Susan had removed it from the box.

Standing at the original glass window overlooking the town, the ripples in the glass slightly distorted the view in some spots. The Blue Mountain coffee was a surprise when delivered to his room. He truly expected just a run of the mill coffee. The croissants, fresh fruit and homemade preserves were a tasty surprise as well.

Knowing it would not be easy to insinuate himself into the community, he needed more information. He was a stranger in town and the citizens always kept their distance until a local vouched for the newcomer. It helped that he ate many of his meals at the tavern. That allowed him to observe the woman who possessed what he wanted and to strike up conversations with the locals. *I believe it's time I approach this young lady and develop a relationship. Maybe she will be willing to share her knowledge if she feels comfortable with me.*

Finishing his coffee, he showered and then descended McCormick Street hill towards town. It felt good to walk along the tree lined sidewalks and take in the fresh mountain air. Mothers were busy sweeping their front porches as youngsters, not quite school aged, played in their very limited front yards. Nodding as he walked by, he was observed with suspicion. *So much for the friendly in "scenic, friendly and busy."* He chuckled to himself. *They might want to think about revising their town mantra.*

Walking past the Baptist church he made his way to Church Street and then over to Rose Avenue. The walk up Ridgeway Street took him to the Bull Pen where the Old Timers swapped lies and assorted stories about days gone by. Having been a regular since discovering that was where the

Old Timers congregated he had ingratiated himself into the club.

Sitting at one of the tables, he sipped the mud they called coffee and just listened, occasionally interjecting a comment or question to feign interest in the topics at hand. Eventually the topics turned more personal and the Old Timers would share the local dirty gossip.

This particular morning, the town gossip was about the missing money from the safe deposit boxes and the death of the bank manager. The conversation then turned to the bank robbery that had taken place in the early sixties. The Old Timers laughed when they shared no one had been caught. Rumors lent themselves to three suspects; a guy by the last name of Nicely was supposed to have been the ring leader. His alleged partners in crime were Johnny Muncy and Roscoe Fitzgerald; all deceased from either old age or suspicious circumstances. One of the Old Timers reminded everyone that the money had never been recovered and it was believed that Nicely had kept it all for himself, but no one knew where he had hid it. Everyone agreed that he had lived like he didn't have a pot to pee in or a window to throw it out of. They all laughed in response to that observation.

Butch noted that all five of the Nicely kids went to college and that took a lot of money with the kids being so close in age. But then Elmer remembered that all of the kids had gotten full ride scholarships; some for sports, some for smarts.

The talk circled back to the murder of the banker. Speculation lent itself to embezzlement along with the stealing from the safe deposit boxes and he was probably murdered by a partner. They all agreed that Billy was odd. Keeping to himself and never being seen with any women except for Becky.

"Wasn't Becky the daughter of Fitzgerald?" Butch asked.

"Nah, I think she was his niece." Grover responded. "But Fitzgerald raised her after her parents got killed in the car wreck not long after the robbery."

Elmer piped up, "Don't ya'll think that's a little strange? There sure were a lot of strange things going on after the robbery." They all agreed.

One of the Old Timers shared that Billy had inherited his family's home after his parents died and rarely was seen in town. Driving by his house at night, many times only one dim light shone from the back of the house. "If he ever dated, it won't nobody from around here."

"I think him and Becky had something going on." Butch observed.

The others nodded their heads in agreement.

Taking care not to appear too interested, the stranger just sat and sipped his coffee taking in every word. The locals had gotten used to him being around and he hadn't given them a reason to be suspicious of his presence. He had hoped that his eavesdropping would give him leads to where the money may be. So far, no luck.

As the hands on the Coca-Cola clock hanging over the bar approached noon, the crowd began to disburse with reasons of "the old lady is probably wondering where I am" and "gotta get my chores done".

~39~

Watching the windows and doors being installed in her new home, Susan was thrilled the interior walls were now in place, as well as the roof and all of the major systems in the house. She just knew it was a matter of time before she would be sitting on her porch listening to the night sounds and the Cow Pasture River flowing by. But, for now, she would have to be satisfied sitting on the grass watching the construction and listening to the pounding of the hammers and the occasional hum of the air compressor.

The death of the bank manager seemed to be a dead end to recovering the missing ten thousand dollars. Every week she would ride to Roanoke to visit her remaining funds just to make sure they were still there. *It's truly sad you can't trust anyone anymore...not even bank managers.* She had decided to take the day off to play construction supervisor and mull over what she knew so far. Sitting with her face to the sun, she closed her eyes to think. The newspapers in Richmond had given her much more information than she expected, but not enough to solve the mystery. The State Library had a large selection of newspapers which truly surprised her since Clifton Forge and Covington were such small towns.

"You on vacation or something?" Cliff stood over her blocking the sun on her face.

Opening her eyes to the shadow, "I'm thinking."

Taking a seat on the grass beside her, Cliff continued, "Yeah? About what?"

"Oh this and that."

"Have you picked out the paint colors and flooring? We're about ready to do that. And you need to pick out the cabinets for the kitchen and the baths."

"Already done, sir." Susan smiled. "Your decorator knows what I want. YOU just need to get it done. I'm tired of living in the inn."

"Well, I would say three more weeks and you should be good to go." Cliff grinned.

Susan almost couldn't contain her excitement. "Really? Three weeks? That is fabulous. I'm so excited!" Leaning forward she grabbed Cliff and gave him a huge hug. "Thank you, thank you, thank you!"

~40~

By the time the bank investigators and the FBI had decided to search Billy's house, someone had beat them to it. Entering the house through the back door, they found drawers pulled out of the kitchen cabinets and left sitting on the counters, rugs pulled up, mattresses overturned, the access to the attic askew and the basement appeared to have been thoroughly searched. Clearly, someone had been searching for something, but did they find it?

Despite the condition of the house, forensics teams were brought in to conduct a thorough search. Instructed to photograph every inch of the house before they began, they lifted fingerprints from every surface, finished opening every cushion and mattress and rechecked every drawer in the house, over, under and behind. Entering the basement they took care to look for anything that would hide a safe, both in the floor and the walls. They also inspected the chimney flue. By the time they were finished with the attic, nothing could have hidden under any of the insulation.

Reporting their findings to Agent Delano, they advised him they were now moving to the three outbuildings. With night falling he felt as if the search of the outbuildings would be useless, but whoever was ahead of them may come back if they have not found what they were looking for.

"I'll have the Roanoke office bring you spotlights so you can keep working. I'll also have them send reinforcements and food."

Two hours later with the sun below the ridge of the mountain that loomed over the house, the last rays of orange sunshine reached for the sky above. Darkness had descended on the land in the shadow of the mountain only to be held back by bright LED lights that turned night into day. Directed toward the exterior of the three outbuildings there was also enough light inside to illuminate every inch of the interior. The surreal scene made the buildings appear extraterrestrial.

Dinner for everyone was also brought in so they could work as efficiently as possible without taking the time to go in search of nourishment. It was going to be a very long night.

News traveled fast about the activities at the Clark home. A crowd began to gather on all sides of the property. Fearing further contamination of an already contaminated scene, Delano called for the local sheriff to provide perimeter control. The two lane roadway had become one lane because of the cars parked alongside. Once the wreckers arrived and began hooking up to cars and trucks on the pavement, onlookers got the message and began leaving. Curiosity was not worth a hundred dollar tow bill. Soon, the forensics team was once again alone except for the lone deputy drawing the short straw to hang around until they were finished.

As the night grew darker and colder, nothing revealed itself. Frustration grew among the investigators who were convinced nothing of substance would be found…until the last building.

Walking across the dirt floor, the sound of muffled footsteps changed to muffled clomps. Kensie, the lead forensics investigator, backed up and listened closely. Again her footsteps went from the sound of muffled footsteps to the sound of muffled clomps. "Guys! I think I got something here!" Taking her booted foot she began to scrape the area that sounded like clomps revealing a plank of wood. "Can someone bring me a shovel?"

Taking the shovel, she began to scrape the remaining dirt from the top of the wood revealing a plank of aged wood measuring approximately two feet by two feet. "Wonder how anyone missed this?" Kensie asked no one in particular.

Lifting the wood from the dirt floor revealed a large round hole lined with corrugated metal. In the bottom appeared to be a large round plastic tub containing another square metal box. "Somebody get me a camera please. And call Delano! We aren't lifting it out till he gets here. "Keep searching," she ordered, "There may be more." With that order, the forensics team began to stomp across every inch of all three outbuildings.

By the time Delano arrived they had found two more boxes buried in the dirt of the other two outbuildings. Photos were taken and care was taken to lift the boxes and tub from the holes. Kensie set to work lifting fingerprints from each before they opened the boxes. Once opened Delano and Kensie were staring at thousands of dollars. "Let's not touch it. We need to get it to the lab to see if we can recover prints or DNA." Delano agreed.

By daylight, the scene had been packed up and cleared with the forensics team and Delano halfway back to Roanoke and their lab. By breakfast at the Bull Pen, the news had spread throughout the town that money had been found on the Clark property.

~41~

The insulation and rubber seals on the metal boxes had protected the contents. The round tubs had stopped the ground water from gaining access to the boxes. Pulling the bills from each of the boxes, the piles were placed in front of their respective containers. Care was taken to not smear any possible prints or DNA on the bills. "Once we process the bills, we can then database the serial numbers to see if they match any stolen from any robberies." Kensie explained.

"How are you going to recover prints from these bills?" Delano, always willing to learn was more curious about the process than the results. A geek by nature, he spent a lot of his time reading scientific journals and attending conferences on the latest and greatest in the sciences.

Kensie enjoyed discussions and debates with him. She felt him to be one of her equals in the world of science and was eager to share with him the latest she learned from her latest training. "Well, there is a fairly new science that has developed a way to detect fingerprints from paper money. Its newest use is money, but it's been in use with non-porous items for a few years. It's called the immunogenic method." This disclosure piqued Delano's interest.

"They've come up with a new method using antibodies instead of sweat and other body fluids to determine fingerprints."

"How does it work?" Delano grabbed a stool and sat down close to the lab table, but not so close that he would be in Kensie's way.

"Well, it seems when we touch something, we not only leave sweat or oils on the surface, but we also leave antibodies. Antibodies don't deteriorate like the sweat and oils, so they can be used in cold cases that are many years old."

Sitting up, Delano was extremely interested now since the money could be from an old bank robbery. "How old?"

"Well, they are still working on that. I need to immobilize the antibodies onto gold nanoparticles and then apply them to a surface. They bind to the antibodies in fingerprints and then I use a fluorescent dye to improve their visualization. I then take a photo of the fingerprint and can upload it into the database to run a match."

"Impressive."

"They say it's really effective for aged or dried fingerprints, even if they are weak. People don't know it, but every time they touch something they leave behind antibodies."

Delano became hopeful that this method would be a break in the current case but also the robbery that took place fifty or so years ago. "So how long will it take before you get any results back?"

"You want all the bills done?" Kensie turned to look at the stacks of bills. "If you do, it's going to take a while. This new process takes time."

Thinking, Delano suggested she do ten bills from each box and then, depending on the results, we may or may not need to do more.

"OK. I'll tell you what. "I'll do random bills from each of the boxes. I'll note the serial numbers and attach the bills to the notes. Give me a few days and I'll holler when I have the results."

Kissing Kensie on the forehead, "Thanks Kensie. You're the best."

"You owe me!" She called after him as he left her lab.

~42~

Two weeks had passed when Delano received the call from Kensie. "You need to come to the lab. We need to talk."

"What's up?

"Just get down here." With that, his phone went dead. Walking the block to the lab, Delano showed his ID to the guard. Being buzzed in, he made his way to Kensie's lab. Hers was one of the few that was not in the basement. Most of the time, her windows were uncovered, allowing sunshine to flood in and occasionally warm the room a little more than she liked. When it did, she pulled the room darkening shades creating a bat cave effect. Today, the shades were partially pulled.

"Whatcha got?" Delano had entered the inner sanctum of the forensics goddess. He always came when she called and said "we need to talk". That always meant she had something good.

Hitting a button on her computer, the display on the large screen across from her table illuminated showing what she had on her desktop screen. "Look at this."

Not sure what he was looking at, Delano waited.

"The prints on the top left are new and belong to Clark, the bank manager."

This did not surprise him. Delano had suspected such would be the results.

"The prints on the top right belong to one Susan Nicely."

"Who is Susan Nicely?" The name rang a bell but he wasn't sure why.

Not having the answer, Kensie continued. "That's for you to figure out. They are also new, just like Clarks. The three prints on the bottom? I'm still running them. They are old."

"How old?"

"Old old." Kensie turned to face him. "I'm guessing at least fifty years old."

"Whoa! Are you serious?" Delano just might have caught a break on the armed robbery. A fifty year old cold case about to be solved? By modern technology?

"Why do you say at least fifty years?"

"Because the years on these bills are in the late fifties and early sixties. Nothing newer. Nothing older."

"This is way cool! Do you think the prints will come back?"

"Depends on if they are in AFIS. You know we didn't start seriously using it until the late eighties. If they worked in banking or some other type of job that required printing, then they will be. Or, if they ever got locked up for anything. But remember, we didn't print back in the day like we print now.

Especially in small towns like Clifton Forge or Covington. Too expensive. I'm running DNA testing now. I'll let you know what I find."

"OK. Let me know if you come up with anything. If not, we might have to take another route." Delano headed back to his office. *This is just way too cool.* He chuckled to himself.

~43~

Deciding to bring the Senior Agent in Charge up to speed Delano made his way to the top floor of the Federal Building. Not one to rub shoulders with the upper echelon he made an effort to stay off of the upper floors. But this! This was something that could really be a feather in his supervisor's cap, solving a fifty plus year old bank robbery.

"Is he in?" Delano addressed his administrative assistant who somehow knew everything about everyone. *She's either a very good spy or has excellent informants.*

Smiling, Jackie turned to meet his gaze. "He is."

"Mind if I step in?" Delano moved toward the door.

Picking up the phone receiver, she punched a number on the dial pad. "Hang on. Let me check." Speaking into the receiver, "Delano here to see you." She hesitated. "Yes, Sir." Returning the phone to the cradle she nodded toward Delano to enter.

"Lin! How are things in the golden tower?" Delano moved toward the SAC extending his hand. He and Lin had gone through the academy together many years ago. Lin had chosen the administrative track, schmoozing and glad handing, while Delano chose the investigative route working undercover assignments, bank robberies and assorted white collar crimes. He enjoyed the thrill of the hunt and catching the elusive criminal.

Taking Delano's hand, Lin grinned. "Good. Good. Same old thing. What's up?"

"I'm thinking I'm about to crack a fifty year old bank robbery," Delano could not hide the pride he felt in this revelation.

"What?" Moving to the chair behind his desk, Lin sat. The news surprised him and he needed to be seated for the story. "Sit. Sit. Tell me everything."

Taking the seat on the other side of the desk, Delano began the story. "OK. So, you know we had the thefts from the bank deposit boxes in Clifton Forge. We also know there was a bank robbery back in the fifties where a hundred and fifty thousand was taken," Delano waited, but Lin said nothing. "Well, I believe we have found ten thousand of the money stolen during that bank robbery all those years ago."

"Really?" The revelation surprised Lin. "That's great. Where?"

"Remember hearing about the bank manager getting killed under Ridgeway Street in Clifton Forge? In one of his outbuildings. I had the forensics team go over his home with a fine tooth comb since it was suspected he was stealing from safe deposit boxes. Someone had been there before us, but they didn't find the money. It was buried in the outbuildings. Kensie found it. Three boxes filled with money. She ran a new test method using amino acids and antibodies to raise fingerprints and recovered five different prints; one for the bank manager, another for a girl who just returned to town and then three unknowns. There were three suspects in a bank robbery about fifty years ago and the money recovered is no older than the early nineteen sixties. I'm thinking there is a strong possibility this recovered money came from that robbery."

Lin sat in silence as he digested what he had just heard. Never in all his years in the Bureau had he heard a story such as this. "So do you have suspects? Do you have any idea where the money has been all this time?"

Thinking for a second, Delano looked at Lin. "Well, Clark and the newest girl in town were both way too young to rob a bank so; it was either their fathers or someone close to them. I can't talk to Clark since someone decided to kill him, but the girl is in town and I plan to talk to her. I want to wait until Kensie finishes the DNA testing on the money and confirms the serial numbers with the stolen money."

"Ok. Well, keep me in the loop. This would be a great coup if you can make arrests and get convictions." Walking around the desk, Lin reached out his hand again. "This is super great news. Keep me posted."

"Will do." With that, Delano returned to his office.

~44~

Visiting the archives stored in the basement of the Federal building was akin to visiting Fort Knox and the gold reserves. After classified information about the Bay of Pigs debacle and the assassination of President John F. Kennedy had been leaked to a couple of well known authors, information that no one had knowledge of unless they had access to the investigative files, Hoover instituted a strictly enforced protocol for access to old files. A protocol deemed a little over the top and much stricter than access to modern day files.

No one could have access to any cold case, or archived files, without express written permission by the Senior Agent in Charge. The request needed to be specific as to the actual files to be accessed and the specific reason for the request. No one was allowed to go on a fishing expedition to peruse files for interesting information. Additionally, two people must be present during the search; the requestor and one other person selected by the SAC.

Any files removed from the archives needed to be signed out by both the agent requesting the files and witnessed by the person selected by the SAC. No files could be removed from the Federal building and no copies could be made of any documents in the file.

Having jumped through all the required hoops, Delano now descended into the basement with Kensie. Lin had chosen her since she was at the scene of the search and had located the money and had been working with the money. She had been pulled from all other cases to concentrate solely on the money case since there was so much of it. Ten thousand dollars was a lot of bills when the denominations were twenties, fifties and hundreds. Her supervisor also pulled another lab tech to assist her.

As the elevator stopped and the doors opened, a slight musty smell assaulted their nostrils accompanied by classic rock filling their ears. Jim Morrison sang of despair about riders on the storm. Dim lighting illuminated rows and rows of government gray, five drawer file cabinets lined up like soldiers waiting to salute a visiting dignitary. Aisles between the rows facing each other were wide enough for two people to walk comfortably side by side. As Delano scanned the room he observed there were five sets of double rows each containing about thirty cabinets. Without doing the calculations, Delano assumed there were about seven hundred and fifty drawers packed with files. Kensie and Delano looked at each other, already feeling defeated.

Approaching from the small office situated to the left of the elevator was a bookish looking young man with pallid skin and a frame too thin for his height. It was clear he didn't spend much time in the sun. "Welcome to the archives." Extending his pallid arm that ended at a small hand with abnormally long, cold fingers, he shook hands with both of his arriving visitors. "We don't get many visitors down here. Welcome."

"Hello. I'm Agent Delano and this is Forensics Investigator Blanc."

"Do you have your form?"

Handing the form to the Archivist, Delano hoped they would not have to search each file drawer. "Can you direct us to where we need to begin?"

"I can do better than that. I can show you the specific place to start. Follow me." Relief filled both Delano and Kensie as they followed the stork like man three aisles over and then to the back of the room. "The years you are looking for are in this file cabinet. We don't have many unsolved bank robberies so we tried to keep them together. The folders are filed chronologically by date starting in the nineteen forties. Be aware that some bank robberies weren't investigated by us. Some local jurisdictions chose to do their own investigations. We needed to be invited in. Some local agencies never did invite us, so some files might not be here."

"OK. Thanks." Delano pulled the drawer open. "You mind if I keep the form? It has our dates on this."

"Uh, let me make a copy for you. We need to keep the form on file. I'll be right back."

Two hours later, neither Delano nor Kensie were having success in their search for the needed file. Concentrating on the robberies in Clifton Forge and Covington, there were quite a few, but only four in the fifties and sixties. Kensie had shared they had recovered ten thousand dollars but none of the robberies were of that amount. There was two where the robbers got two thousand, another for five thousand and one for nine thousand, but nothing for ten thousand or more.

"Wonder if the local PD decided to investigate the robbery themselves?" Kensie wondered aloud.

Looking up, Delano thought for a moment. "If they did, why would they have the FBI investigate these small robberies?"

"Maybe someone with the PD was involved in the others?" Kensie questioned. "I don't know."

"Or maybe the money we recovered is a mixture of funds taken during more than one robbery? We need to take the list of serial numbers."

"You know we can't do that. We either have to take the whole file or nothing at all. No copies. Sorry, Delano, I'm not getting jammed up over making copies." Kensie smiled.

Grinning, Delano pulled out his phone. "The policy said we couldn't make copies. It didn't say we couldn't take photos." Snapping photos of the serial number lists for each of the four files, they returned the files to the drawers and returned to the office of the archivist.

"Any luck?" He came around his desk.

"No. Nothing definite, but maybe some leads."

Extending his boney hand, "May I see your phones please?"

Shocked at the request, Delano hesitated. "I don't have mine." Kensie replied.

"You sir?" The stork waited with his hand extended. "We don't allow any copies made of any of our files. It's in the policy. And photos are equal to copies as far as the director is concerned."

Busted, Delano opened his phone to the photos and deleted them. "Guess we need to take the entire file?"

"Yes, Sir."

And with that, Kensie and Delano returned to the cabinet containing the files of interest and retrieved all four. Carrying them back to the archivist, he logged them out, counted the number of sheets of paper and stamped each one with a tracking ink to ensure the files, or any of the papers, did not leave headquarters. Handing the files back to Delano, he then had them sign the documents outlining the policies concerning borrowing the files and an oath acknowledging they would be prosecuted if any of the information found its way outside of approved channels.

"Well, that was interesting." Kensie was the first to speak once the elevator began to ascend. "Hoover must have really gotten burned on the Kennedy and Bay of Pigs information." Delano nodded.

Exiting on the lobby floor Kensie headed toward her lab to determine if her assistant was able to compile the serial numbers. If not, she would lend a hand.

Delano continued on to the fourth floor and his desk. He needed to secure the files before he made calls to the Clifton Forge and Covington police chiefs to set up meetings. There had to have been more robberies.

~45~

Although the two chiefs were new to their positions, they were willing to do what they could to help with the investigation. The lack of trust of federal agents had faded over the years and the newer generation of local law enforcement was more willing to open their files and work alongside the Feds. First stop would be Clifton Forge.

Chief Craft hailed from Virginia Beach. Having been born in Clifton Forge and taken to the coast by his parents as a baby, he had chosen to return to his roots, to a slower life. Having risen through the ranks with the Virginia Beach Police Department, he had taken the opportunity to not only work closely with other police departments in the area, but had built relationships with ranking personnel in the various branches of the military that called Hampton Roads home. He had also worked closely with the numerous federal agencies that called the area home. Considered a progressive chief, Delano couldn't help but wonder how long he would last in this small sleepy town, far from the glitz, glamour and action of the big city.

The conversation went well. The chief brought in his captain in charge of investigations, David Patterson, who had been with the police department for twenty years and was a native of the area. His knowledge of the community was priceless in shedding light on the robberies investigated by the police department without the help of the FBI, as well as the rumors that had circulated over the years.

Divulging that the latest talk about the murder of Clark had resurrected the rumors of the robbery of Mountain National Bank back in the sixties piqued Delano's interest. "Do you have a file on that robbery?"

Pointing to the file on the desk, Patterson started, "I thought this would be of interest to you. A hundred and fifty thousand dollars was taken during the robbery and there were three suspects. No arrests were ever made and interviews were conducted. I made copies of the file so you can take it with you."

"Thank you. This will be a great help." Taking the file from the desk, Delano began to flip through. "Is there a list of serial numbers of the bills taken?"

"There is a partial." Patterson confirmed. "Not all were listed, but I'm thinking what is there should help you compare, or at least get a sense if the money belongs to this robbery. By the way, they only reported to the press that one hundred thousand was stolen."

"Why was that?"

"According to the file they were hoping to get someone talking. They figured if the real figure hit the gossip mill they could track down the source of the original amount."

"Did it work?" Delano asked.

"Obviously not since no arrests were ever made." Patterson laughed. "Guess whoever got the money didn't feel the need to correct the amount."

Standing to leave, Delano thanked the chief and captain for their assistance. He then headed for Covington.

~46~

Stopping by the tavern for a late lunch, Delano decided to peruse the file shared with him by the Clifton Forge Police. The meeting in Covington wasn't productive at all. Not that the chief wasn't cooperative, but Delano got the feeling his presence wasn't welcomed. Although the chief was new, he came from a smaller town and didn't particularly care for federal agents. He too had brought in his Investigations Captain, however, he had nothing to share.

Flipping through the file, Delano found the list of suspects; Howard Nicely, Roscoe Fitzgerald and Johnny Muncy. *Wonder if any are still alive?* Just then his Spicy Tavern Burger arrived along with a tall glass of amber stout. "Can I get you anything else right now?"

"Uh, yeah. Did you grow up here?" Delano was looking for anyone who could shed light on the whereabouts of the three suspects.

"Sorry. No," responded the waiter.

"OK. Thanks." Delano attacked his burger with a vengeance. Having not eaten since breakfast, the interviews had taken longer than expected. Coupled with the drive from Roanoke, his stomach was thinking his throat had been cut and would never be introduced to food again. It announced such on the drive from Covington.

The late afternoon hour brought more of the older locals into the tavern. Delano decided to slow his progress on his food and focus his hearing on the assorted conversations around him, hoping the topic would be the death of Clark and the old bank robbery. He wasn't disappointed. As the alcohol flowed, the speculations began. Those who had clearly been born and raised in the area were full of conjectures as to where the money had come from. Talk turned to the Mountain National Bank robbery in the sixties and the coincidence that the long forgotten incident seemed to pop back into the news about the same time that Susan Nicely decided to return to town.

Susan Nicely? Delano flipped through the file to the suspects list. Nicely was listed. *There are tons of Nicelys in the area. Hell, they even named a town after them.* Interrupting the conversation at the next table, he moved closer. "Uh, excuse me. Do you mind if I talk with ya'll?"

"Who are you?" The older gentleman wearing the C&O cap asked.

Flipping his credentials so all could see, Delano identified himself as the agent investigating the death of Billy Clark and the discovery of the money.

"Pull a chair up, Sir." The two couples slid their chairs over making room for him to join. Delano pulled his chair over and brought the remains of his meal and his folder with him. "What can we do for you?"

"Can you tell me about the Mountain National Bank robbery…and about Susan Nicely?"

"Sure, sure," the man in the cap agreed. "The bank was robbed in 1962. There were three fellars who walked in with shotguns and demanded money. Right at closing. All the money was in the vault so they just had to grab bags from in there from what I heard."

Not to be outdone, the second man interjected. "I hear they got about a hundred thousand, but nobody ever said definite. Nobody got caught either," he chuckled. "Man, I would've liked to got that money." The others laughed.

"Now what would you do with all that money, Lester?" The lady that appeared to be Lester's partner touched his arm. Delano couldn't see if she wore a wedding ring or not.

Grinning, Lester responded. "I'd buy us a place in Florida so we could get out of these cold winters."

Surprise filled her face. "Oh you would, would you?"

"Yea."

Interrupting the dreaming, Delano asked about Susan Nicely.

The C&O capped man answered his question. "She's the daughter of Howard Nicely. They lived down on the Cow Pasture. Down off forty-two."

Making notes on the inside of the folder, Delano sought an address but no one was able to give him one. Just like every local in town, directions were by landmarks, not addresses.

"Ain't it down by that church that sits down at Carter's Place?" The lady who had remained quiet during most of the conversation finally spoke. "They own all that land down in the bottom. Well, at least the kids do now."

"I hear tell Susan is fixing up the house and moving back," Lester spoke. "I hear Cliff is doing the work." Just then Cliff entered the tavern. "Well, there's Cliff now." Everyone turned to see a tall construction type walk through the door. "Hey Cliff! Come here!"

Following introductions, Cliff shared that he had been building a house for Susan and was now finished. "I believe she's moved in now." Sharing the address with Delano he then excused himself to find a seat at the bar. Pulling out his phone, he dialed Susan's number giving her a heads up about the FBI asking questions about her.

"OK. Thanks." Susan disconnected the call and turned to examine the hole she had made in the sheetrock in her bedroom closet. A hole that would eventually hold a wall safe that would contain the money. The move into her own home had finally given her a sense of security. Now, all she needed to do was to get the money within her control and all would be good. *I hope.*

The lone stranger everyone had become used to sat close enough to Delano and the group he was talking with to hear every word of the conversation at the table. Thanks to Cliff's disclosure he now knew who this Susan was and where she lived. Now, he just needed to find her.

~47~

Driving south on two twenty, the setting sun brought a glow to rainbow rock and a surreal appearance to the flat lands that stretched between the hills. Dusk filled the stretches of roadway that had lost the sun making sunglasses unnecessary. The steady stream of cars northbound brought residents of Clifton Forge, Covington and the surrounding areas home from their jobs in Roanoke; one of the few places to find gainful employment for those who didn't wish to work on the railroad or at the paper mill. Their other option was to cross North Mountain into Lexington. Employment options with a livable wage were better in Roanoke; thus the steady stream of cars and trucks southbound in the morning and northbound at night.

The hour ride was no big deal to anyone living in Roanoke or Clifton Forge. Delano had gotten used to it in the past few months since the bank manager had been found dead and the money had been found at his property. Since it was believed the missing money and the dead bank manager was connected, Trooper Putnam was happy to turn the entire investigation over to the Feds. Thankful not to have to make the drive daily, Delano didn't mind the every other day or whatever the investigation called for. He knew it was only a matter of time that the drives would end…at least for a while.

~48~

Waiting for Delano when he logged into his computer the next morning was a spreadsheet of serial numbers for the money recovered at Clark's property. Listed in three columns, Kensie had been kind enough to sort them numerically from least to most. Unfortunately, the list the police chief had given him wasn't. It was a handwritten list in no particular order. Thankfully there was a search option on the spreadsheet which Delano planned to use hoping to speed up the process.

Kensie arrived about thirty minutes into the tedious job of comparing serial numbers. "Whatcha doing?" Sitting on the corner of his desk she turned to look at his screen. "Oh. Having fun?"

"You know it." Delano grinned. "Ya wanna help?"

"Not really." Kensie smiled. "I've seen my fair share of these numbers."

Hoping she was teasing, Delano persisted. "What else do you have to do?"

"Uh, hand you the report of the touch DNA for the body."

Surprise filled Delano's face. "What? It finally came back? It's about time!" Taking the report from her, he began to read. DNA recovered by Alice from the body matched Clark and an unknown subject. That subject was female. "Did you run it against the touch DNA on the money?"

Not wanting to spoil the surprise, Kensie encouraged him to keep reading. Watching with anticipation she wanted to see his expression on his face when he read the match wasn't exact, but it was familial. "Familial? What the hell does that mean?"

"It means that whoever killed Clark is blood relative to whoever touched the money at some point in time."

"What? You mean to tell me that the person who killed Clark is the same person who touched the money sometime between the time is was printed until it went into those boxes on Clark's property?"

"No. That's not what I'm saying." Frustration filled her face. *These agents! They use the technology, but they have absolutely no idea what it means.* "You know how they use familial DNA to track down homicide cold case suspects by submitting DNA to those DNA sites everyone uses for their genealogy?" Delano nodded. "Well, it's the same concept. Whoever left DNA on the Clark body is related by blood to someone who handled the money found in the boxes."

"So, has the DNA been submitted to the DNA sites?"

"Not yet. We're attempting to recover enough to submit that isn't tainted. When we do, we'll get a list of any family members that have used the service. The problem is, there are at least five different services so we are going to have to submit to each. And there is no guarantee that anyone from that family has submitted a test. It's going to take about a month to get the results after samples are submitted. Oh, and the SAC has to sign off on the submissions."

"Ok. Well, let me know when you get anything to submit. In the meantime, ya wanna help me with this fun project?"

Hesitantly, Kensie agreed to help. "Email me the spreadsheet and give me a list. Whose desk can I use?"

"Use Keacher's, he's on vacation."

As the clock hands moved toward and then past noon Delano and Kensie made progress on the lists. The majority of the numbers from the boxes were matching the lists provided in the police file. By quitting time they had finished the tedious chore and both were exhausted.

Standing and stretching, Kensie complained that her body had stiffened with all the sitting. Bending over, she touched the floor with her palms while not bending her knees. She held that pose for two minutes trying to stretch the muscles in her back, her spine and her hamstring. "Oh my gosh I'm stiff!" She declared. Standing erect, she then stretched to her right from the waist with her left arm over her head and then reversed the action to the left.

Watching this activity, Delano felt a little guilty not having the desire to stretch. *I guess I've been a couch potato a little too long. Maybe I should do something about it.* "You wanna go get something to eat? Maybe something to drink?"

Continuing the mini-workout Kensie agreed to the suggestion. "You buying?"

"Oh yea. I owe you big time." Delano agreed. "If it wasn't for you, the list would never have been finished…at least not for a few days. Where you wanna go?"

"How 'bout the Blue Five? They have great beer, great food and music. Plus, we can walk there."

"Let's go." Locking the files in his desk and shutting down the computers, they headed out, grateful for fresh air and exercise.

~49~

Days had passed since Susan received the heads up from Cliff about the FBI agent. Using the time wisely, she focused on getting the safe installed. Pleased with her work she was ready to retrieve the money from the safe deposit box at the bank. Walking from room to room she was thrilled about being home. Maybe not the home her father had built and she grew up in but it was still home; in the same location and she knew her parents' spirits were with her.

Pouring a glass of wine, she decided to sit on the deck and listen to the river. The sound told her that the river was high. Rains had come to the higher elevations and the drain-off now passing her land would soon join the James River and eventually spill into the Chesapeake Bay. *Such a peaceful way to live. I'm so glad I gave up the DC rat race. I can still make money remotely and retain my sanity.* An uneasy feeling came over Susan as if she was being watched. Listening closely and looking around she heard and saw nothing, but the feeling would not leave her. Moving inside, she decided to pull the curtains blocking the view of anyone or anything that might be out there. *I'm so glad Dewey convinced me to put up curtains.* Switching on the TV she decided to catch the news while she fixed dinner.

~50~

Having followed the directions overheard at the tavern, the stranger found the new construction at Carter's Place. Confirming his find through the property records, he knew this was the Nicely place. The area wasn't the best for surveillance since it was sparsely populated and mainly flat farm land in a bowl. He would have to either sit up on the roadway leading into the area, park in the church lot or sit on the side of the mountain in the trees. The first two options could draw unwanted attention to him and someone might call the law on him. The third didn't thrill him, but he felt he could stay longer without being detected. The thought of sitting in the woods did not appeal to him. He might have mountain blood coursing through his veins but he was city raised only returning to this area as a youth to visit grandparents. Visits that were infrequent at best once his parents divorced.

Cleaning out his mother's house upon her passing, the stranger had found a diary hidden behind a shelf full of books. Pages yellowed and writing faded with age, he strained his eyes to read the words written so long ago. Being drawn into the revelations, he knew there was more to what he read than the information on the three or four pages he scanned. Securing the diary in his car he made sure it was hidden from his siblings as they cleared the home and prepared it for sale. Once alone at his beach front home, he opened the diary and began a journey through the secret life of his parents.

Page after page spoke of the angst his mother felt about his father's activities. Activities that were considered borderline illegal even by mountain standards. He could hear the desperation in his mother's words as she worried about the company he kept when he occasionally returned to his hometown. She worried about the safety of her children and the security of their future if he was ever caught for the things that he and his buddies did while she stayed in the flat lands near the coast. He became so absorbed by the words his mother wrote, the sun had dipped below the horizon making it difficult to see the faded words.

Now he found himself back in the mountains of his birth; an area strange to him. His grandparents' homes reminded him of the few times they had visited. The theatre brought back memories along with the City pool and Douthat State Park. But these were distant faded memories of days gone by. His return was prompted by cryptic words written by his mother about his father as well as two of his buddies: Roscoe Fitzgerald and Howard Nicely. She wrote of the disappearance of a large sum of money and the suspicion that Nicely had helped himself to all of it. The anger of her thoughts was palpable and seemed to sear the pages they were written on. She expressed the feeling of being cheated and felt that retribution was necessary. Included in the diary was a yellowed newspaper clipping of the bank robbery. It appeared the money had vanished and no one was ever arrested. Paul Muncy had returned to recover what was rightly his father's and to give rest to his mother who died carrying a burning feeling of being cheated.

~51~

Sitting in the church parking lot, Paul watched the house through binoculars. Appreciative of the fact that the curtains remained open most of the time and the windows were virtually floor to ceiling he was able to see the majority of the interior of the home. Convinced she was living alone, he thought about approaching under the pretense of contemplating building in the area when a red truck drove by and parked outside the Nicely house.

Mounting the steps two at a time, the male driver knocked as he opened the door. "Anybody home?" he called.

"Dewey!" Susan moved quickly toward her favorite brother giving him a super hug. "I'm so glad you are here." She squeezed him again.

Hugging her back and lifting her from the floor he twirled around. "OK Mutt. Give me the nickel tour."

"With pleasure!" Assuming the air of a model, Susan led him through each of the rooms waving her arm with entry into each room and pointing out what she felt were the highlights. With the tour ending in the kitchen, Susan opened the fridge retrieving a Guinness for Dewey and pouring it into a glass. Grabbing a glass of wine she suggested they move to the deck overlooking the river.

After catching up, the conversation turned to the money...as it always did. "I understand the FBI are in town and they've been asking about me," Susan declared. Surprised Dewey asked how she found that out. "Cliff told me. Evidently he was at the tavern while the agent was in there snooping around."

"So where is the money?"

Jumping up, "Currently in the bank. Come see." Susan grabbed Dewey's hand and drug him into her bedroom. Opening her closet she pushed her clothes to the side revealing a long narrow door that blended in with the wall. Pressing the door it opened toward her reveling an industrial gray metal slab with a key pad recessed into the door. Pushing four numbers and then touching a small dark circle with the pad of her ring finger above the keypad she pulled the recessed handle opening the gray slab to reveal a recessed vault.

"WOW! You've thought of everything haven't you?" Clearly impressed, Dewey never thought his sister would think of recessing a vault inside the wall of her closet. He definitely didn't think she would think of using a double locking system; keypad and fingerprint identification. "So, who else knows about this vault?"

"No one." Susan proudly exclaimed. "I did it myself. Once Cliff and his crew finished the construction and he got the occupancy permit, I did the vault."

"Have you changed all the locks on the doors?"

"I have." Susan was so proud of herself she could barely contain herself.

"What about an alarm system? Is the box watertight in case the place floods?" He was just full of questions.

Closing up the vault and returning the hidden door to its location to hide the vault, she turned to Dewey. "Being installed next week and yes, it is. Come on. Let's go sit on the deck before the mosquitoes come and run us inside."

~52~

The newspaper headline announcing the discovery of the money on Billy Clark's property infuriated Becky. She knew he had the money. She knew he was lying the day they met at Douthat. *Damn it! I should have known by the way he was acting when I confronted him. Now the money is gone. But where is the rest?*

Finishing her breakfast, she put the dirty dishes in the dishwasher just as she heard tires crunching the gravel in her driveway. Not expecting anyone, she went to the window and saw Gary's truck pulling into the backyard. Exiting the truck, he smiled when he saw her open her backdoor. "Why are you here?" Standing on the porch with her hands on her hips, she wasn't pleased to see Gary on her property. He too had been a disappointment when he failed to recover the money for her or get Billy to tell him where the money was; money that was buried within fifty yards of the house.

"Well good morning to you." He stopped his approach. Hoping he would be welcomed as he had been in the past, it was clear from the tone of her voice he wasn't. "Can we talk?"

"I don't know if there is anything to talk about." Becky didn't move.

Stepping onto the lower step of the porch, Gary began, "I think there is. We need to talk about what has happened and where we go from here."

Acknowledging that fact, she invited him in, inviting him to sit at the kitchen table. "What more is there to talk about? You failed. The money is gone and we have no idea where the rest is."

"You need to know that the FBI has the money." Gary began.

Picking up the paper laying on her table, she shook it at him. "Don't you think I know that?"

"I know you know what you've read in the paper, but I know more."

Becky stopped. "What do you know?"

"I know they are doing DNA testing on the money and they are using some fancy testing to lift fingerprints from the money." Gary began.

The news set Becky back. "How do you know this?"

"People talk."

"What people?"

"Just people."

Gary's response did nothing to calm Becky. In fact, it enraged her even more. "Look. If you're here to play games then just leave. I don't need games and I definitely don't need your crap. If you had done your job when you went to visit Billy that money would be ours and we would know where the other money is. But no! You couldn't even do a simple job." Pacing back and forth to contain her rage, she felt an almost uncontrollable urge to attack him.

Trying to control his anger, he needed Becky to calm down, but the last thing he wanted to do was to tell her to do so. He knew it would just set her off even more. So he waited for the rant to end. Once it did, he began.

"There's talk around town that the FBI are using some new science to find out who touched the money and who killed Billy. I don't know much about it, but they say there is some kind of DNA test."

Becky listened. "What kind of DNA test?"

Shaking his head, "I don't know. All I know is people are talking about DNA testing."

"So?"

"So. Where have you been? Haven't you seen those shows on TV about solving crimes using DNA?"

"I've heard about it, but I don't understand it."

"Neither do I, but supposedly they can track down suspects and convict them based on their relatives. Something about all those DNA tests people are using for genealogy. You got anybody into genealogy?"

"Not that I know of," Becky started to think. She had submitted her DNA to some site about ten years ago. Somebody was tracing their maternal line and her cousin talked her into taking part in the test. Reluctantly, she did. "Now how they gonna get DNA from money?"

Gary shook his head. "I don't know. Magic I guess. All I'm saying is they got ways of doing things so maybe it's good we didn't find the money."

The rant started again. "Have you lost your ever lovin' mind?! If we had found the money they wouldn't have! Good lord Gary! Think!"

"Well. Just keep your ears open. I'll let you know if I hear anything else." And with that Gary left slamming the door as he went. *I don't have to take abuse from that witch. If she was so hot to get her hands on the money, she should have done it herself. Ain't no pleasin' her.* Backing out of the driveway, he put the truck in first gear, hit the accelerator and popped the clutch leaving acceleration marks half way down the road. Becky watched from her living room window.

Booting up her laptop she decided to do some research on this DNA he was talking about. Carrying her computer to the kitchen table, she poured herself a cup of coffee and sat down to begin. By lunch she knew everything she ever wanted to know about DNA use in law enforcement including tracking suspects through DNA banks normally used for genealogical research. *Well, I don't have to worry about that. My DNA won't show up on the money since I never found it and it definitely won't show up on Billy's body.* She laughed out loud.

~53~

A month had passed since Alice and Kensie started their magic with the DNA. Lifting the DNA from the body was a cinch. Always was. The money, on the other hand, proved tricky because of the age of the paper, but they were able to lift enough to send to all the DNA sites normally used by genealogists as well as to run it through their very own database for comparison to known criminals. Not wanting to get Delano's hopes up, Alice waited until all the results were in before she summoned him to her lair. By the time he arrived, she had all the results displayed on her wall monitor including possible local connections. Having worked as a Medical Examiner for more years than she cared to admit, Alice didn't mind sharing the work load with Kensie when it came to DNA, but she wanted to give Delano the results.

"Glad you brought breakfast." Alice smiled. "Did you bring me some?"

Delano grinned, "You know I did." Setting two bags on the counter, he started pulling chicken biscuits, fruit and coffee from each. By the time he finished, there was quite a feast spread before her.

"Wow! Are you hungry?" she grinned.

Confirming her observation, he also voiced that he believed this would be an all morning session since he wasn't as educated as she was about touch DNA. "Let the schooling begin."

"OK." Alice began. "Let's start with the DNA recovered from the murder scene." Alice moved the mouse on the laptop which brought her wall screen to life. Staring down at them were the vacant eyes of Billy Clark, bank manager. "William Luther Clark, age forty-three at the time of his death. Worked at the bank as the manager and lived in his parents' home he inherited when they died. Cause of death was, he got his ass beat bad." Alice couldn't help but chuckle. She always wanted to say that as a cause of death. This time it was true. Delano laughed. He couldn't help himself. "Well, actually he died from the head wound and the ass beating."

"Any DNA on him that didn't belong to him?" Delano was learning…slowly.

"Some. Enough to test, but no matches in CODIS. The bruises match somebody's fist, but it appears that whoever kicked his ass was wearing gloves. And they were really, really mad."

Surprised at that last statement Delano asked her what caused her to draw that conclusion. "Because his cheek bone and eye socket were broken and it takes some serious force to break the cheek bone. I believe a fist did the damage and that fist was attached to a powerhouse body that stood between five eight and five ten."

"Do you think maybe he was slammed into the pilings for the bridge? That could have done some damage."

Impressed, Alice agreed, but pointed out that if the entire face had slammed into a piling, the forehead would have been damaged which it wasn't.

Clicking the mouse, the screen changed to display fingerprints. "Now to the money. After Kensie removed touch DNA from the money we then developed the fingerprints. Taking ten bills from each of the three boxes, we recovered a boatload of prints. What you see are the six that are most prevalent. There is no way for me to tell which are most recent so, I just went with the ones that showed up the most. The top three and the one on the far left are all unknowns. The center bottom and bottom right are knowns."

"Knowns? Who do they belong to?

"The one in the center belongs to a Susan Nicely. She's a securities lawyer from D.C. The one on the right belongs to our dead guy."

"So, I'm assuming since you know who the last two are you ran them through AFIS?"

"I did."

"OK. What about touch DNA?"

"I've submitted all the DNA to the assorted genealogy sites and I'm just waiting for the results to come in. Once they do, then I can start putting the puzzle together. Oh, and by the way, Susan lives just outside Clifton Forge off forty-two." That fingerprint revelation put Susan front and center on his radar.

"Yea, that's what the locals told me. Thanks Alice." Delano finished his biscuit and grabbed his coffee leaving the rest for Alice to either consume or share. "Keep me posted on what you find. Got places to go and people to talk to." With that, Delano was out the door and headed to Clifton Forge yet again.

~54~

The drive to Carter's Place gave Delano time to think. As with every investigation with no witnesses, it was slow going. Putting a jigsaw puzzle together with all the pieces the same color blue would be easier than this. *I got ten thousand dollars in cash buried at the dead bank manager's house, prints on the bills that belong to four unknowns, a dead guy and a girl with the same last name as one of the suspects in a fifty year old bank robbery. Interesting how their prints showed up on bills taken during that robbery.*

Pulling up to the house on the Cow Pasture River, it was clear that it was a new construction; brand new. A little red convertible sat to the side of the porch accompanied by a red pick-up. Mounting the steps, Delano knocked on the door. No answer. He knocked again. Hearing voices coming from the other side of the house, he walked around to the back to find a thirty something auburn-haired female talking with a like-colored hair man. Carrying lawn chairs and a cooler, it was clear they had been sitting in the river relaxing. Not being noticed by either, he spoke stopping both in their tracks.

"Can I help you?" Susan was the first to respond. She also had the feeling she had seen this guy before but was unable to place him.

Displaying his credentials, Delano introduced himself and asked to talk with Susan privately.

"We can talk in front of him," nodding toward Dewey.

"Have we met before?" Delano immediately recognized her from the bank during the safe deposit checks. He waited to see if she remembered…or would acknowledge it.

Thinking for a second, Susan didn't acknowledge they had ever met. "Have you ever worked in D.C.? I just moved down from there."

Not acknowledging her question, Delano asked if they could talk inside. He was hoping to get a look at the interior.

"I prefer not. What do you want?" Dewey had hung back allowing Susan to take the lead. After all, it was her house. No introductions were made except for Susan and Delano so he felt no need to introduce himself. Walking toward the house, he chose to give them the privacy Delano wanted. Susan had hoped he would stick around as a witness.

Realizing she would not make things easy for him, he began. "I'm investigating the homicide of Mr. Clark, the bank manager. I believe you and I met during the safe deposit box inspections." He waited. Susan did as well. "Was there anything missing from your box?"

Shifting her stance, "No. There wasn't. Why?"

Not wanting to divulge what he knew about the money just yet, he continued. "We're just double checking. It seems that Mr. Clark had a second set of keys to the boxes and it's believed there were items taken."

Susan's BS meter was pegging all the way over in the red alert zone. "I thought that was why we were summoned right after Mr. Clark disappeared. Wasn't it?"

"It was, I'm just double checking."

"Well, everything in my box was still there. Look. I need to get out of these wet clothes." Ending the conversation, Susan mounted the steps to the back deck.

"Well, thank you for your help." Sarcasm was clearly present in his statement. "I'll be in touch." Noting the license plates of both vehicles before driving off, Delano headed back to Roanoke. Feeling stuck until the DNA results came back, he decided to research the three suspects in the robbery…hopefully with Kensie's help. Paul watched as the Fed left the cabin.

"Kensie. I'm headed back to the office. Are you available? I need to do some genealogy research on the robbery suspects and could use some help.

"Sure."

"I'll be there in about forty-five minutes."

~55~

Hearing the knock on the door, Susan was perturbed. "What is this, Grand Central Station?" Grabbing her robe she padded toward the door. "What? You can't answer the door?"

"Hey! It's your house," Dewey pointed out as she opened the door. She glanced back at him with the "you're a pain" look.

"Can I help you?" A tall dark haired, well muscled and tanned specimen of a man stood at her door. Standing about six two with deep blue eyes, Susan's mood instantly changed and she pulled her robe a little tighter.

The wide smile revealed a set of perfect teeth that looked like the owner had never eaten anything that would stain them. "Hi. My name is Paul. I'm looking to build in this area and was riding around looking at different houses. I noticed yours and it looks like it was just built."

Impressed with what she beheld, Susan confirmed his impression.

"Can you tell me who your contractor was?"

"Cliff Burke. Burke Construction. He's in Covington.

"You mind if I look around?"

"Sure. Go ahead." As he stepped forward to enter the house, Susan stopped him. "Sorry. Not inside. You can look around the outside."

Feigning embarrassment, Paul apologized as he stepped back. "Sorry. I just thought you meant I could look around inside."

"Nope. I don't know you. Sorry." Stepping outside Susan continued. "I'll be happy to answer whatever questions you have out here.

~56~

Kensie's fingers were flying over his keyboard by the time Delano arrived at the office. "It's about time you got here" she grinned.

"Hey! I got here as soon as I could. Whatcha doing at my desk?"

"What you asked me. Look. I got the full names and dates of birth for Nicely, Fitzgerald and Muncy. And I got their high school photos."

"How'd you do that?"

"Magic." Her fingers kept pressing keys.

Looking at the photos attached to the front of the files, one face stared back at him. A face looking vaguely familiar. "Who's this?"

"Nicely."

An hour ago, Delano had met a slightly older but more recent version of the face staring at him. "I believe I met his son. Does he have a son?"

"Well, that is a very good question. I'm still researching that. Census records from nineteen fifty on haven't been released yet so I'm having to go around the back way." Stopping for a second, she turned to face Delano. "Did you bring me something to drink?"

"I did." Setting a grande iced mocha latte on his desk he moved to pull another chair up so he could sit and see the screen. Picking up the other two folders he asked who the others were.

"This one is Fitzgerald and this one is Muncy." Pressing the print key, she picked up her latte taking a sip and then headed for the printer. "Be right back."

The papers Delano was handed contained information about Nicely; his addresses, known family members, date of death and where he currently rested. "You got all this on the computer?" He knew there was more than anyone wanted to be published about themselves on the web, but what Kensie had just handed him was enough to create a fake identify. "You know, this is really scary."

"I know. Right?" Kensie sat down in front of the computer and began retrieving the same information for Muncy and Fitzgerald. By the time she finished she had retrieved the census records for nineteen forty along with newspaper articles mentioning each of them. There was only one article mentioning the bank robbery and it listed all three of the men as suspects.

Reading the information, Delano found a glaring discrepancy. "Wait. You sure this address is right for Muncy?"

Swallowing her sip of latte Kensie confirmed the information. "Yep. Those addresses are straight from the DMV files."

"But it says Muncy was living on the Peninsula at the time of the robbery."

"Yeah. And?"

"So why would he come all the way to Clifton Forge to do an armed robbery? I'm sure there are plenty of banks down on the coast he could have robbed."

"And that's why you get paid the big bucks," Kensie grinned. "Look. You said this wasn't going to be an all day thing and I'm getting hungry. It's almost two o'clock. Let's go get something to eat. Besides you owe me."

"I owe you? I bought last time." Delano stood, unlocked his desk drawer and slid the folders along with the papers in the drawer and relocked it.

Appearing to be miffed, Kensie pointed out that without her he never would have the information she gave him in such a short period of time. "Hell, if I had left it to you and your research, you'd be sitting here till the cows came home. Now come on. Buy me lunch." Heading for the door she knew he would follow. He always did.

~57~

Deciding to hit one of the local food trucks, they took their feast to a park bench allowing them to continue their conversation about what Kensie had discovered. To an outsider the pair appeared to be a father and daughter meeting for lunch even though Kensie was just ten years his junior. They also appeared to be at opposite ends of the spectrum when it came to life philosophies; he in his dark suit and tie, she in her calf length batik print dress and strappy ankle boots. Impressions couldn't be further from the truth. They were both committed to their professions. He was so committed it had cost him his wife. Having tired of the long hours his investigations demanded, she left never giving him a hint that she was leaving. Or, maybe he just missed all of the hints because he allowed his job to consume him. He would never know since she was killed in an auto accident before their divorce was finalized.

Kensie preferred the free and single life. Whenever she chose to vacation, she could, as long as she had the time on the books and no cases demanding her attention. Forensics fascinated her. She would spend hours reading cold cases and attending the latest training. Eternal love had evaded her several times, the most recent when death took her fiancé.

Scuba diving in Turks and Caicos off a live aboard, he had participated in the night dive and became disoriented. Descending deeper than he should he developed nitrogen narcosis and continued to descend deeper. His body was never recovered which left a huge hole in Kensie's heart and tons of unanswered questions. Thus, she threw herself into her work while she built a wall around her heart to protect herself from ever being hurt again.

"So, how did you come up with all that information in such a short period of time?"

"I told you. Magic," She grinned.

"Seriously." Delano took a bite of his fish taco. "I'm amazed."

"I just used a couple of premium sites we have access to and then I searched the newspapers on the State Library site. They highlight search terms so it makes it easy to scan quickly. Then, someone in their infinite wisdom decided to put a lot of the high school yearbooks online."

Delano shook his head. "Why would anyone do that?"

"Because everyone wants to know everything. This veggie taco is really good. Thanks."

Swallowing the last of his fish taco, Delano nodded.

Continuing, Kensie explained that she searched the yearbooks for Clifton Forge, Covington and Central High not knowing where they lived during their high school years. "It turns out Nicely and Fitzgerald went to Central and Muncy went to Clifton Forge. It's unusual for county kids to hang with city kids, but I guess they were unusual. I just wish I had access to later census records. I need to search the ancestry site online to see if anyone is researching those lines. That will be beneficial when the DNA results come back for the touch DNA." Delano did not respond. "Are you ok?"

Looking a little dejected, Delano hesitated. "I just feel like I'm falling behind. I've been an agent going on twenty years. When I first started, using DNA was a maybe. Maybe a match would come back. Maybe the courts would accept the science. Now? Now you just have to touch something to transfer DNA and science can find you through your relatives. I knew about the websites that could find addresses and reverse phone numbers but finding suspects by connecting their relatives who innocently ran their DNA through some genealogy website? That just blows my mind. I need to check into some training."

"Are you feeling like a dinosaur?"

"I am. You ready to go back to the office?"

Standing, Kensie turned to face Delano. "Let's go for a walk." Gathering their trash she deposited it in the nearest trash can. "Come on."

Walking through the park, Kensie did her best to convince Delano he was not a dinosaur. Explaining that technology is making advances by leaps and bounds into areas never before seen at this speed, no one was capable of keeping up. "By the time the information is published, tested and accepted by the judges, it's already outdated. Privacy no longer exists."

Nodding, Delano agreed. "That's an understatement. I just know that I need to attend more training and thank goodness I trust you and Alice to keep me straight."

"Stick with us. We'll keep you straight. Let's head back to the office and check those ancestry sites. I'll let you do the work. I'll be your guide." Taking her hand Delano thanked her for her encouragement. Kensie appreciated the human touch of someone who wasn't stone cold dead.

~58~

Deciding to use what Kensie had taught him, Delano dug into Howard Nicely's background. He visited the Clifton Forge courthouse where the will was probated and learned that there was not only Susan and Dewey but also three additional siblings. Searching their names, he learned one lived in Florida, another in California and another in Arizona. Dewey lived at the beach. *So, Dewey was the only one who apparently lived close enough to visit Susan on a regular basis. Wonder if he found out that Clark had stolen the money from Susan's safe deposit box and beat the crap out of him to find out where he put it? A theory. All I got right now is a theory.*

Kensie had guided him through the ancestry site for Muncy and Fitzgerald revealing that Fitzgerald had a living daughter. Nothing showed up for the Muncy clan. Searching the internet, Delano found a Rebecca Fitzgerald living in Covington. *I'm betting that might be his daughter.* He then searched the school yearbooks and found her photo. Printing it out, he compared it to her father's photo. There was a slight resemblance, but not enough to say she was definitely his daughter. Jotting down her address below her photo, he decided he would make a visit the next time he headed that way. For now, he would wait until Alice confirmed more information with the touch DNA. *This was going to be an educational case to say the least.*

Reading the newspaper articles mentioning the Three Musketeers; aka Muncy, Fitzgerald and Nicely, he learned they had each played football for their respective high schools. The team Muncy had played with won the one A State Championship. The paper published photos of the team with each player identified underneath. Delano printed the photo. He also discovered the three had been arrested for breaking and entering with several other people. Evidently, there was a gang roaming the area that broke into stores stealing a variety of items. They also stole new tires from vehicles at the local Ford dealership. All had received probation and apparently completed it successfully.

Entering their adult years, the three appeared to have cleaned up their acts and stayed out of trouble…or at least didn't get caught. Howard Nicely was featured in a feel good article in the Daily Review about his donations of food to the community. It was noted that although he and his wife were raising five children on a farmer's income, he made sure to bring a station wagon full of fresh vegetables to the town center every Saturday. If people couldn't pay, he would just give them whatever they needed. *Well, that was very philanthropic of him. How could a man put five kids through college, scholarship or not, and still manage to give enough food away to make the newspaper? Not all scholarships cover all costs.*

Fitzgerald had joined several of the fraternal organizations in the area. He had also served in the military for four years after graduation. Returning to the area, he had married and had a daughter, the one Delano assumed was the Rebecca Fitzgerald living in Covington. He had also gone to work at the paper mill and played on their softball team. This was confirmed by the nineteen sixty photo of the team, all smiles holding a large trophy.

Search as he may, no articles in any of the local papers mentioned the third Musketeer, Johnny Muncy. No engagement announcement, no marriage, no death, nothing. It was as if he just vanished from the area after graduation. *Where did you go Johnny Muncy?* As if on cue, Delano received a text from Alice. "Come see me. DNA is back." Forwarding the text to Kensie, he asked her to join him at Alice's adding that he wanted her in from the beginning so she could help Alice educate him.

~59~

"Hi guys! Ya'll ready to be schooled again?" Alice enjoyed company. People rarely came to visit unless they were summoned. Science can be a lonely pursuit.

"We are." Delano acknowledged. I brought back-up to hear first hand what you have to say so she can hear what I miss.

Feeling somewhat put off, Alice began her education of Delano…and Kensie. She liked Kensie, but she was hoping to have Delano to herself for a while. "Well, as you know I was able to obtain six touch DNA samples from the money. We already had identified the fingerprints of Clark, so I didn't bother to test his any further. I ran the other five through CODIS and got a hit on one…Susan Nicely which I expected since she is the securities attorney. A few years ago, after the big financial bubble burst, the Securities and Exchange Commission started requiring anyone involved in securities submit a DNA sample, just in case." Delano nodded his head. "Susan matched two of the unknowns from the money. Both are male so I did the lineage test on them and determined one is a brother and the other is her father. Didn't you say she had four siblings?"

"Yes," Delano confirmed. "There were a total of five Nicely kids. From what Kensie and I have determined, the only one that lives close enough to be in town is a brother a year older than her. Dewey, I think is his name. I saw him at her house the other day. Looks a lot like his father."

Continuing, Alice shared she had gotten a partial match on one of the unknowns with a known in CODIS named Paul Muncy. Taking those two samples I ran a high stringency test on them and got a positive familial hit. The lineage test shows that Paul Muncy is the son of the unknown. You'll need to do some digging around in the ancestry sites or other databases to confirm that they are related and what the unknown's name is."

Kensie interjected that it's probably Johnny Muncy. He was one of the three suspects in the bank robbery back in the early sixties. "But, why is Paul Muncy in CODIS?"

Alice grinned. "You are never going to believe this. He was arrested for unauthorized use of a kayak," she laughed.

"A what!?" Neither Delano nor Kensie could believe what they heard. "A kayak?" Delano laughed. "This guy has a record and DNA in the system for taking a kayak for a ride?"

Still laughing, Alice confirmed his statement. "Evidently in Virginia if you take a horse, aircraft, vehicle, boat or vessel without the owners consent and get caught, your DNA goes into CODIS. And according to Virginia law, a kayak is a boat." Laughter filled the room at how ridiculous the law was.

"Isn't that a bit of an overreach?" Stating the obvious, Delano couldn't stop laughing.

"Ya think?" Kensie was laughing so hard she could barely speak.

"So which jurisdiction made this dangerous arrest and put this criminal's DNA in the system?" Delano was still laughing.

"Virginia Beach."

Trying to get serious again, Alice shared that there was also a familial match to the last unknown. "Evidently, a girl named Rebecca Fitzgerald took a DNA test years ago, like when they first started this genealogy testing, and her DNA is still in the system. The last unknown is her father. So you have a CODIS match for Susan Nicely and DNA matches to two males, and you have a CODIS match for Paul Muncy and a DNA match to his father. Both of those matches have been confirmed by lineage testing. Then you have a DNA site match for Rebecca and an unknown touch DNA on the money who is definitely her father according to the lineage testing. Now, your job is to take what I gave you and find out which one of the wonderful humans killed Clark and where the rest of the money is."

Standing, Delano thanked Alice for the information and the additional work load.

"Glad to help." Alice grinned and began closing her program.

As Kensie and Delano started for the door Alice asked Delano if she could talk with him for a second. "Sure. What's up?" Kensie stopped, waiting for Delano to accompany her back to the office. "Go ahead" Delano directed Kensie. "I'll catch up with you." Kensie glanced disapprovingly at Alice and headed back to the office.

"What's up?"

"Would you like to have drinks after work?" Alice moved closer to him taking his hand. "You seem to have more questions about my results. I thought maybe we could have drinks and I could help you understand this new technology a little better."

"Yeah, that'd be great. I'll see you at five?"

~60~

Returning to his office, he found Kensie on his computer surfing an ancestry site. The temperature was a lot cooler between them than it was before the DNA briefing. She was more professional than usual and answered his questions with short responses. Rising from his chair, she went to the printer, returning with a stack of papers. Handing them to him, she gave him a broad overview. "According to someone named Joe Fitz45, Rebecca Fitzgerald is the full blood daughter of Roscoe and Vera Fitzgerald. The dates of births and deaths for Roscoe and Vera are on the chart. She is also the half-sibling of Gary Fitzgerald and Clifford Burke. I couldn't find any divorce information for Roscoe and Vera; so, it appears that Roscoe might have had a wandering eye that he clearly followed with his body."

Clueless, Delano asked if Kensie was ok.

She continued. "I found a tree that includes the Nicely clan. It appears that Susan is the youngest of the five kids. Her siblings, we already know about. Her parents are both deceased and reside at Mountain View Cemetery. Oh, by the way, the Fitzgeralds reside at Cedar Hill Cemetery and Mr. and Mrs. Muncy reside at Parklawn Cemetery in Hampton. As far as I know, everyone else is still alive and kicking.

Look. I gotta go. Got a call. I think I got you enough to move forward in your investigation." With that, Kensie left quicker than he had ever seen her move.

He was completely perplexed as to what had come over her. Checking his watch he saw it was quarter to five. *Time to go meet Alice.*

~61~

The evening was a combination of fun and work. Enjoying their tapas and margaritas, conversation began as work and the methodology of DNA and its evolved to more personal topics. Delano shared his divorce story and how difficult it was to meet someone new working long hours. Alice too commiserated about the long hours and the difficulties of having a life outside of work.

They learned they had a lot in common besides the job; camping, the beach and salsa dancing. Alice shared there was a new salsa club that had opened in the old market building. Suggesting they go, Delano checked his watch. It was early. "Sure, why not?" Paying the check, Delano helped Alice from her high stool. Just as he turned to lead her out, Kensie appeared. "Kensie!"

"Hello Kensie." Kensie's appearance did not please Alice. She had hoped to have Delano to herself for the entire evening. Hoping to bed him, the last thing she needed was a little girl getting in her way. "What are you doing here?"

Smiling at Delano, Kensie turned to face Alice. "Same as you…getting something to eat." The smile directed at Alice looked more like a smirk. "Are ya'll leaving so soon?"

"We are." Turning to Delano, Alice took his arm. "Are you ready?"

"Sure. See you tomorrow Kensie."

Arriving at Viva Havana the music was rocking when Delano and Alice walked through the doors. Several couples were on the floor moving to the beat. Hands were becoming familiar with their partners and the hips swayed to the rhythm. The personal temperature was rising and the music kept thumping. Grabbing Alice's hand, Delano led her to the dance floor and began to move his hips. She followed his lead and they soon embraced allowing the distance between their bodies to close to mere inches. Their bodies moved with ease together. It was clear to them both that the movement would translate well to the bedroom. Margaritas flowed and so did the conversation when they weren't dancing. Laughter filled the space between them and neither could stop from touching the other.

The night ended with them doing the horizontal salsa at Alice's place. Confirming what they both knew on the dance floor, the chemistry continued in the bedroom. So much so that they awoke the next morning in each other's arms.

"Good morning salsa queen." Delano smiled as she opened her eyes to see him already dressed, buttoning the last buttons on his shirt. "I need to go. Need to shower and I have court at eleven." He bent over her and kissed her forehead. "See you later?"

She smiled and agreed. "Looking forward to it." She heard her door close as a huge smile spread across her face. *Oh my. He is as good as I always thought he would be.* She giggled to herself. Not wanting to shower because it would remove his musky scent, she knew she must. Fixing breakfast, she continued to glow as she rewound the events of the night before. Heading to work, she knew she wouldn't be able to wipe the smile from her face and others would key in on her changed demeanor. She was lighter…less stressed. *Oh it's been so long. I really needed him last night.*

~62~

With another conviction under his belt, Delano returned to his office. He needed Kensie to help him navigate the ancestry websites, but she was nowhere to be found. Hoping she would show, he decided to make some phone calls.

Calling the Clifton Forge police chief, Delano secured an interrogation room to use when he was ready to question the Nicelys and the assorted Fitzgeralds. He wasn't sure if there was a need to question Mr. Muncy, if he was even in town. That might call for a trip to the Beach. Only time would tell.

Hanging up the phone he looked up to see Kensie entering the room. "Hi! Can you help me with the ancestry sites? I need to look at those trees."

"I printed them out for you. Didn't you look at them?" Her voice was frosty.

Unlocking his desk drawer, he pulled out the folder. Opening it, he flipped through the papers until he found the family trees from the site. Reading over the information it appeared that someone named Fitzgerald had published his tree for public use. It confirmed what Alice had told him about Roscoe and Vera. The tree only showed one biological daughter for the two. *Wonder if she knows she has brothers?* He needed to find the brothers and take a look at them.

Whoever killed Clark was strong, powerhouse strong according to Alice, and stood between five eight and five ten. The guy at Nicely's house appeared strong but not powerhouse strong and his height was just outside the window. *Wonder how angry someone would need to be to hit someone so hard it would break their cheek bone?*

"Kensie, can you show me how to log into that site and search it?"

"Sure." Delano pulled up a chair so they could sit side by side. Kensie sat, but there was a definite chill in the air. "So, how was your night?" She pulled up the site and bookmarked it for him. "You need to use your department log in and it will open you to the search page. Go ahead. Log in." She didn't even pretend to turn her head as he logged in. She watched every keystroke. Taking over the keyboard, she showed him how to search and to limit the searches. She also showed him how to save the results in his own box and also how to print all the results he received.

"This is amazing. You can dig and dig through every aspect of someone's life." Delano was amazed. "There are no secrets any longer."

Standing, Kensie confirmed his observations. "Look. I gotta go. Let me know if you run into any problems."

"Thanks. Lunch later?"

Kensie stopped. "Uh, I'm busy."

"I didn't say what time." Delano pointed out.

"We'll see." Kensie turned and left the office. She could tell he had had a long night. A night she knew had been spent with Alice. Kensie wasn't sure if she was jealous or sad.

~63~

The auburn-haired beauty sitting across the table from Delano in the Clifton Forge interrogation room was a contradiction in her appearance. The auburn upswept hair gave the air of a big city, sophisticated girl, but her boots, jeans and plaid shirt screamed down home country girl. Either could handle herself depending on the situation and Delano knew it. Having worked in the DC headquarters for eight years, he had interacted quite frequently with Northern Virginia lawyers trying to make a name for themselves. Knowing that Susan was a securities attorney and had worked for one of the largest firms in the Washington metro area, he was not going to assume anything…except she could hold her own.

The light in the room was lacking in brilliance. The one light fixture overhead clearly belonged to the decade in which the building had been built. The lone naked bulb hung from a long clothed electrical cord. *Wonder if that's a fire hazard?* The solitary window clearly had not been washed in several years…probably because it was on the second floor and faced another two story building across the alley, which further dimmed any sunlight that may try to visit from the outside.

"Thank you for coming in Ms. Nicely." The video camera had been activated prior to their entry allowing him to catch every word, every action from the very beginning. Susan had taken the seat he offered across from the camera.

"No problem. Is this about my safe deposit box?"

"Would you like something to drink?"

Susan immediately knew his answering her question with a question, no matter how insignificant, meant there was more to this meeting than her safe deposit box. She immediately stiffened and took on the persona of an attorney. "No thank you."

"I understand you just returned to the area?"

"Yes." Consciously deciding to only answer the specific questions asked, she also decided it would be best to limit any details given. *I need to not show any surprise or emotion.* Having been on the other side of the table, Susan was well versed in the games played by investigators. She was also well versed in the signals given by defendants with their body language. Knowing she had not done anything wrong, she was unsure as to what this agent wanted with her. *Did this have something to do with the money?*

"You grew up in the area?"

"I did." Susan confirmed. "Look. What is this about? I'm very busy."

Delano explained that he was investigating the robbery of the Mountain National Bank in the sixties and the death of William Luther Clark, the branch manager of the Alleghany

National Bank here in town. "You were one of the people who had items taken from their safe deposit box, no?"

"No." Susan unconsciously shifted in her seat.

Continuing, Delano asked if she had a personal relationship with Mr. Clark.

"Look. Let's just cut to the chase Mr. Delano. What exactly do you want with me? I'm a very busy person and I'm not going to play your silly games."

Opening the file in front of him, "Look, Mr. Clark was found dead under the bridge for Ridgeway Street."

Shifting again, Susan answered, "I'm aware."

"So why would someone kill him?"

"How would I know?" Susan stood to leave.

Standing to block her departure, Delano cut to the chase. "Your fingerprints were found on money that was stolen from Mountain National Bank in the nineteen sixties. Care to explain?"

The statement stopped her in her tracks. Hesitating, she looked directly into Delano's eyes. "Well, considering that I wasn't old enough to rob a bank then, I would say that someone has made a mistake."

"I don't believe so, Ms. Nicely."

"Am I being detained?"

"No. Not at this time." Delano stepped aside. Susan could not leave the room or the building fast enough.

Driving back to the cabin she called Dewey who did not answer. Being cautious not to leave a voice mail, she decided she would call him later. The paper had reported that the money had been found buried at Clark's house. She needed to research how much evidence they could recover from fifty year old money. *I guess I should have worn gloves touching the money, but who would have thought to? I need to get the money out of the bank in Roanoke and stash it in the vault immediately. They could get a search warrant for that box and take all of the money.* Pulling onto the roadway leading to the cabin, she saw Dewey's truck sitting outside. Relief filled her as she parked beside it and entered the cabin. "We need to talk." Susan announced to Dewey before she even saw him.

"Hello to you." Dewey came from the kitchen carrying a beer for him and a glass of merlot for her. "Where have you been?"

Taking the wine; "talking to an FBI agent." Susan plopped down on the sofa and pulled off her boots.

"Why?" Dewey sat in the overstuffed chair across from her. He grabbed the remote and clicked on the fireplace. Susan looked at him.

"Is the fire necessary?"

"For me it is." Dewey smiled. "It relaxes me."

"Well, wine relaxes me." Taking a sip, she continued. "And I need to relax. Seems my fingerprints were found on the money they found at Clark's house. And if they found mine, I guarantee you, they found yours too. The agent has done his background and he knows the money came from the robbery back in the sixties. He also knows that you are my brother."

"Hell, everybody knows that. It's no secret. We did grow up together ya know."

"I need to go get the rest of the money and put it in the vault. If they find out I have a safe deposit box anywhere, they can get a search warrant for it and my prints on that money gives them cause to search my place."

"You want me to go with you?" Retrieving another beer and the bottle of wine from the kitchen, Dewey topped off Susan's glass.

Nodding, she confirmed she would. "Carrying that kind of money, I would rather you would. I was nervous as all get out walking to the bank with it."

"OK. We'll go tomorrow. You wanna grill something?" Susan padded to the kitchen in her sock feet. "I think I want a burger. You?"

~64~

Becky Fitzgerald was more forthcoming than Susan when she came in to speak with Delano. Sharing that she and Clark were friends, she was devastated by his death. Not able to think who would want to harm him, she assured Delano that everyone liked Billy.

"Your father was Roscoe Fitzgerald?" The question caught Becky off guard.

Regaining her composure, she acknowledged he was. "But he passed away years ago. Why do you ask?"

"Can you tell me about your brothers?"

"Brothers? I don't have any brothers? I'm an only child." The question confused Becky.

Delano continued knowing he had thrown Becky off her game. "Are you sure?"

"Of course I'm sure. I would know if I had brothers." Shaking her head, Becky couldn't see where this agent had gotten that information.

"Ms. Fitzgerald, do you know anything about DNA testing?" Knowing she did, he waited.

Nodding her head she spoke of taking the DNA test many years ago at the request of a guy who was tracking his maternal line. Not able to recall the name of the DNA company, she shared that she only knew her DNA was able to confirm his research and a woman who lived around Waynesboro had been a ninety-nine percent match. "Maybe that's where you think I have brothers."

"No ma'am. It isn't. Your brothers aren't related to your maternal line. It's your paternal line. Your father."

"That can't be." Clearly Becky was shocked at the disclosure. "My parents had a happy life and Daddy would never have run around on her."

Sliding photos of Gary Fitzgerald and Clifford Burke in front of her, he asked. "Do you know these two men?"

Staring at the photos, she began to weep. "Are these my brothers?"

"Do you know them?" Delano persisted.

"Yes. I went to high school with them. Gary was two years behind me and Cliff was in my grade. Are you saying these guys are my brothers?" A tear rolled down her tanned cheek. Delano waited.

"They can't be my brothers. My Dad would never…" Becky's voice trailed off into silence.

Feeling sorry for her, he continued. "Look. You said you were familiar with the DNA testing. You admitted submitting your DNA to a genealogy site." Becky nodded. "Well, do you know anything about touch DNA?" Looking at Delano with a confused look, Becky had no idea what he was talking about. She wiped her eyes with a tissue provided by Delano and shook her head. Providing what little information he understood about touch DNA, he actually sounded like an expert to her. Explaining they had recovered her father's fingerprints and touch DNA from the money recovered at Clark's house, they were able to take that information and connect the dots to show Becky had two half siblings; Gary and Clifford. Silence filled the room as Delano waited.

"So, tell me. Why would Gary or Clifford kill Clark?"

"What? They wouldn't." Becky insisted. *Hell, Gary couldn't even get the money back from Clark. He sure didn't have the balls to kill him. And Cliff? He knew nothing about the money…at least I don't think he did.*

"Then can you tell me why Gary's fingerprints were on the knife block in Clark's kitchen?"

This revelation surprised Becky. *Maybe he did have the balls. Why else would his fingerprints be on the knife block?* "I have no idea. Maybe they were cooking?"

As the afternoon passed into evening, Delano could feel the cat and mouse game being played by this witness. Or was she a suspect? *She certainly didn't appear to have the strength to kill Clark.* Realizing he was getting nowhere, Delano suddenly thanked Becky for coming in. Advising her he would be in touch, he escorted her to the door of the police station. Watching her drive away, his gut told him she knew more than what she was saying. *I believe Gary needs to be the next interview. I need to get Kensie to pull up all calls and texts on Becky's phone. That is, if she's still speaking to me.* Thanking the chief for the use of his interrogation room, he advised that he would be using it again the next day.

~65~

"Good morning, Kensie." Delano was headed north toward Clifton Forge to meet with Gary Fitzgerald. The frost in Kensie's reply caused a feeling of frostbite in his being. "Are you ok?"

"I'm fine." The frost continued. "What can I do for you?"

"Look. I'm headed back to Clifton Forge to interview Gary Fitzgerald. Can you survey the banks in the Roanoke area and find out if any of the people we've identified have a safe deposit box? Also, find out when it was opened and when it was last accessed?"

"Sure." Kensie responded curtly. "Anything else?"

"Uh, yeah. Can you pull the phone log for Becky Fitzgerald and Gary Fitzgerald? I'm specifically interested in the time period about the time the safe deposit box investigation started and when we found Clark's body."

"Sure. Anything else?"

"No. I think that will do it for now. Thanks." Disconnecting the call, Delano couldn't understand why Kensie was being so frosty. Clearly something had happened, but he had no clue what it was. The ringing of his phone interrupted his thought. Answering without looking at caller ID he was pleasantly surprised to hear Alice's voice.

Smiling into the phone, Alice began, "Good morning. Are you coming in this morning?"

"Not till the afternoon. What's up?" Remaining professional, he never knew when his phone was being intercepted.

"I was able to size the fist that took out Clark. Took some fancy science, but I finally got it. Can't make a cast of it because there is no real indentation but at least you'll have an idea of the size of the hand."

Unaware this could even be accomplished; Delano was surprised at the disclosure. "So, how wide is the hand?"

"Well, considering the punch it packed, it's actually pretty small. If I didn't know better, I'd say it was a woman's hand."

"WHAT? I thought you said it was a powerhouse of a man." Confirming Delano's statement, Alice stated that the powerhouse of a man had women's sized hands or it was a woman who was really, really strong. "So how wide is this hand?"

"Between three and a fourth and three and a half inches. Remember, we need to adjust for the gloves."

"But gloves can't add that much width," Delano observed.

Concurring, Alice reminded him that she needed to take it into account. "Oh, and by the way, I found a small piece of dark brown canvas between his teeth."

"Uhm. Now that's interesting. How small?"

"Just barely there."

Changing the subject, Delano asked if Alice knew what was bothering Kensie. "Why do you ask?"

"Well, she seems a little frosty."

Alice smiled. Knowing exactly what her problem was, she declared she had no idea. "Look. I got another call. See you later?" With that the call was disconnected.

Arriving at police headquarters, Delano watched who he thought was Gary Fitzgerald mount the front steps. Taking his time to follow, Delano wanted Gary to wait. Waiting always made suspects nervous.

~66~

Two hours later, Delano had gotten Gary to admit that he knew Becky. He also admitted that he had been at Clark's home but couldn't remember the last time.

"So, do you cook when you're at Clark's?"

Gary's reaction was one of confusion. "Why would I cook at his house?"

"Maybe you were lovers?" Knowing this comment could elicit an angry response, Delano waited.

The tall muscular farmhand just stared at him. No emotions showed on his face and there was no shift in body language. Gary just sat there staring. The response was far from what was expected. Delano continued to wait. Watching him, Delano observed the muscles defining the chest under the tight t-shirt and in his arms. The hands, clasped together on top of the table were smooth for a farmhand. They also appeared to be small for a man the size of Gary.

"Do you wear gloves when you work?"

The question seemed to jolt Gary from his daze. "Of course."

"Where are they?"

Confusion filled his face as he shifted in the chair and sat on his hands. "Why do you ask?" Remembering what Becky had told him during their conversation last night, Gary thought he was doing a good job of giving no hints about himself.

"Just wondering. You mind if I take a look at them?"

"Why?"

"I'm a city boy and I'm thinking about buying a farm." Delano lied. "You look like someone I could learn from and was wondering about the best kind of gloves to buy."

Not buying his story, Gary declined. "They aren't in my truck."

"Where are they?"

"What is the interest in my gloves?" Gary was truly confused. "I thought this was about the money ya'll found at Clark's house." Delano did not answer.

Looking at his watch, Gary stood. "Look man. This is wasting my time. I got work to do."

"Have a seat sir."

"Look. Sounds to me you're just fishing. I ain't got time to fish. I got work to do. You're burnin' daylight and the sun will be setting before I get my work done." Remembering the three magic words Becky had told him to be able to walk out, he continued. "Call my lawyer." With that, Gary walked out leaving Delano with a surprised look on his face. *Clearly I under estimated this country boy. I got nothing* to hold him on and no reason for a search warrant for his truck since he didn't say his gloves were in there, I just gotta let him go for now.

Well, that's three for three. I need to talk with Dewey if he's in town. I'm sure that's who was at Susan's the other day. Thanking the chief for the use of the interrogation room, Delano was backing out of his parking spot when his phone rang. "Delano."

"Agent Delano." The familiar voice on the other end was still frosty.

"Hi Kensie."

Getting straight to the business at hand, Kensie disclosed that Becky had a safe deposit box in Clifton Forge at Alleghany National Bank. Susan and Dewey were co-renters of a box in Roanoke at the Blue Ridge National Bank. "It seems Becky opened her box about two years ago and hadn't been in it in a while. Susan and Dewey opened their box the day after you started the investigation into the thefts from the boxes at Alleghany."

The news did not surprise Delano. Both Susan and Becky were strong suspects in the money case, but neither seemed to be strong enough to punch Clark hard enough to kill him. "So when did Susan or Dewey last access their box?"

"This morning."

Pulling onto Carter's Place, Delano saw only one vehicle parked at the cabin, the truck. Exiting his vehicle he mounted the steps to the porch and approached the door.

Hearing a vehicle approaching from behind, he turned to see the little red MG coming down the dirt drive that ran along the property of the church. Waiting, he saw both a man and woman in the vehicle. Parking beside the truck, Susan exited the car along with Dewey.

Extending his hand, Delano began, "Good afternoon, Ms. Nicely. Agent Delano."

"I remember." Susan responded curtly. "What can I do for you?" She did not shake his hand. "Ladies don't shake hands."

Turning to face the male, "Are you Dewey Nicely?"

"I am."

Clearly topping six one, Dewey was about the size of Gary. Both muscular, both tanned., but Dewey was more slender than Gary. Extending his hand, Dewey shook it. "That's a powerful grip you have there, Mr. Nicely." Dewey did not acknowledge the compliment…or was it an observation?

Withdrawing his hand, he continued to the porch following Susan. Delano thinking he would be invited in followed along behind. Suddenly, Dewey turned toward the porch chairs offering Delano to have a seat in the chair that placed his back to the house as Susan continued inside. Taking the chair across from him, Dewey waited for Delano to begin. Susan proceeded to draw the curtains blocking the view into the house if Delano decided to turn around.

Breaking the silence, Delano began. "So, do you live here with your sister?"

"No."

"How often do you visit?"

"Why are you asking?" With his sister being an attorney, she had already told him about the interview with Delano and had prepped him on how to respond to any questions. She also told him she would be his attorney, if he was charged with anything, until they could locate a really good criminal defense attorney. Of course, neither knew what he could be charged with, but with the Feds, you just never knew.

"Look. I'm sure your sister has already shared with you the information about the money. We believe Clark took the money from your sister's safe deposit box and you also touched it according to touch DNA."

Impressed with the revelations, Dewey responded. "Well, it appears you've been quite busy. Am I being charged with anything?"

Delano ignored Dewey's question. "Do you own canvas gloves?"

Dewey repeated himself. "Am I being charged with anything?"

Susan was just inside the door listening to the conversation. She was also recording it on her phone. The second time Dewey inquired about charges; she stepped out onto the deck with her phone in hand. "Mr. Delano, you are well aware I'm an attorney, correct?"

"I am."

"Then you either need to answer my client's question as to whether he is being charged, or you need to leave."

Not wanting to end the conversation, Delano confirmed that neither Dewey nor Susan were being charged.

"Then it appears you are fishing." Susan observed. "Therefore, I need to ask you to leave."

Being accused of fishing for the second time, Delano was not pleased. "I know you are, or have been, in possession of money stolen from a bank robbery in the nineteen sixties." Susan and Dewey both laughed.

Susan responded. "Neither of us were born then, much less old enough to rob a bank. If that's all you got, I think you need to leave." Susan walked to the top of the steps leading to the yard and waved her arm in a way that directed Delano to leave. Delano did as requested not seeing the smiles on Dewey's and Susan's faces since they were behind him.

Waiting until his vehicle was up the hill and way out of sight, Dewey retrieved the satchel from the trunk of her car. Carrying it inside, Susan followed. "Take it to my bedroom. We'll put it in the safe." Doing as instructed, Dewey placed the satchel on her bed. "I'll open the safe. Go ahead and pull the curtains."

"He's gone and I truly doubt anyone is sitting on the mountain watching us."

"Better safe than sorry," Susan replied as she motioned for him to pull her curtains.

Disappointment filled Becky and Gary as the opaque curtains closed, blocking their view. They had been sitting on the side of the mountain watching through binoculars long enough to see Delano's arrival and subsequent departure. "You know he's just fishing don't you?" Becky broke the silence between them. Gary did not reply. "Did you know we were siblings?" Gary continued to remain silent. "Did you?" At least fifteen minutes passed as Becky awaited a response. "You knew didn't you?"

Gary finally turned to look her in her eyes. "I suspected." No explanation followed. Becky waited.

"What made you suspect?"

Gary looked at her. "Well, look at us. Have you ever looked at pictures of us side by side? Like in the school yearbook?" He waited. Becky did not respond. Changing the subject, Gary asked. "What do you think is in the satchel?"

Becky turned back to the house, "I'm betting it's the rest of the money."

Surprised at her response, Gary pursued her thinking. "Why do you say that?"

"Why wouldn't it be? She couldn't trust Alleghany Bank to keep the money safe so, what makes you think she would trust any bank?"

Gary nodded. "How do you know there is more than the ten thousand?"

"Clark told me there was." This revelation surprised Gary. "He said there was actually a hundred and fifty thousand dollars total. I think he only took the ten thousand because he didn't think it would be missed."

Gary chuckled. "Boy was he wrong. But why in the world would she put it in her house, though? The floor wouldn't support the weight of a huge safe."

"But wouldn't the walls?" Becky turned to face Gary. "If it was me, I'd have a safe installed between the studs and have the studs reinforced to support the weight.

Impressed, Gary was amazed that Becky had given this a great deal of thought. "Do they make safes to fit between studs?"

"They do. We need to talk to Cliff. Maybe he'll tell us if he installed a wall safe."

Shaking his head, Gary doubted it. "You know Cliff keeps everything to himself."

Becky looked at him. "Maybe to himself, but not from his siblings."

This revelation made Gary laugh. "What? You gonna claim he's your brother to get him to talk?"

"He's yours too." The laughter stopped.

"No way."

"Way."

Seeing everything they could see, they decided to go to the tavern. If they arrived at the tavern soon enough they could get a table near the door and maybe Cliff would show up. The drive into town was educational for Gary. Not only had he found a new sister, he also learned he had a brother. All of them had believed they were only children. "Boy were we fooled," Becky laughed half heartedly.

~67~

Warmth had not returned to their relationship by the time Delano returned to Roanoke. Kensie was at her computer researching another case when he entered her lab. "Hi. Got anything for me?" Kensie handed him a manila folder without speaking a word. "Ok. Thanks."

Taking the folder, he headed for a desk in her lab. Ensuring he was facing in Kensie's direction, he began to review the information she had discovered for him while glancing occasionally over the top of the file.

"Why are you here?" Kensie was feeling uneasy with Delano hanging around.

"In case I have a question."

"You could call."

"I could," Delano agreed. "But, if I hang around long enough you'll tell me why you've been so frosty towards me lately."

Kensie shook her head. "It doesn't matter."

"It does to me."

"Look. I got work to do. You need to go to your office. If you have a question, call me…on the phone." Delano stayed where he was continuing to read the file.

It appeared that Becky and Gary maintained constant contact from the time the thefts from the safe deposit boxes was investigated up until, as recently as, last night. There were also conversations between Becky and Clark. *Now, I know she knew Clark, but did she know him well enough to contact him after office hours...or even on his personal cell?*

The reports on box ownership really didn't surprise him. Becky had a box at Alleghany National Bank and so did Susan. But Susan and Dewey also owned a box at Blue Ridge Bank in Roanoke. *Now why would she need two boxes?* Not accessing her box since long before the investigation, Delano knew he could rule Becky out. Susan, however, was another story. She had accessed her box at Alleghany just a couple days before the investigation and then opened the box in Roanoke the day after she was called in to check her box for theft. Delano's gut was telling him he knew where the remaining hundred and forty thousand dollars was, but he still didn't know who murdered Clark. *The motive was the money. I know that. But who killed him?*

Looking up from the file, he saw Kensie appearing to wrap up her research. "Would you like to go get a drink?"

"I'm busy."

Laying the file on the desk, he walked over to hers. Sitting on the corner of her desk he looked at her. "Can we talk?"

"Sure." Kensie was gathering her papers and shutting down the computer.

"Did I do something to hurt you?" His look of confusion was real.

"No." Kensie stood to leave.

Grabbing her wrist, Delano didn't want her to leave. "Look. Whatever I did to hurt you, I'm sorry. Problem is, I don't know what I'm sorry for."

"Kensie's look was one of unbelief. "Really?"

"Really."

"It doesn't matter." Pulling her wrist away from his grasp, she took the file she had been assembling and left the room. "Have a good night."

As Kensie walked out, Alice walked in. "Hi handsome!" Kensie stopped. She then shook her head and continued to leave. Alice smiled to herself. "You ready?"

Unsure what Alice was talking about, Delano was perplexed? "Ready for what?"

Embarrassment filled Alice's face. "I thought we were going out."

"Uh, no. I'm going home." Delano suddenly realized what he was in the middle of. There was a subtle cat fight going on for his attention. He had never experienced anything like this. Always the regular Joe, he had never been someone the girls fought over. He worked out a little to keep his blood pressure down, but not enough to be considered buff. Not an action type of guy, he was more cerebral than athletic. Now he understood the chill from Kensie. Having taken her hand in the park, he unknowingly sent a signal he was interested in her. He was, but only professionally. She was way too young for him. Alice was closer to his age, but she was a co-worker. Learning years before in his career, he would never dip his wand where he made his green. He realized he had made a huge mistake the other night. *Maybe it was the tequila. Maybe the salsa. Doesn't matter. It won't happen again. Hell, my career and a friendship aren't worth a piece of ass, young or mature.* Leaving the office, taking the file Kensie had assembled for him, he headed home.

~68~

With the money secured in her brand new wall safe, Susan suggested they celebrate with steaks on the grill. "What are we celebrating?" Dewey was confused.

"That we have the money and no one can take it from us," Susan smiled as she headed for the kitchen. "Why don't you start the grill? I'll grab the steaks from the fridge and get us something to drink."

Always one to follow instructions, Dewey headed for the back deck. Seeing movement in the trees across the river, he stopped. The animals in the mountains always fascinated him. Not wanting to come face to face with one, he still enjoyed watching them from a distance. But these were not animals. It was people. Humans. Dewey watched as the two humans moved through the woods toward the swinging bridge. Grabbing his phone he attempted to take pictures. *Why would these humans be in those woods? There's no reason.* Calling Susan, he pointed at what he was seeing across the river.

"That looks like Becky." Susan exclaimed. "Why would Becky be across the river on the side of the mountain?" Not waiting for a response, "Who's that with her?" Calling out, "BECKY!" she attempted to elicit a response from the girl on the side of the mountain. The girl looked in her direction. She then tucked her head and pushed the male ahead of her. He stumbled. "Who's the guy?"

"I don't know. They're headed for the swinging bridge. Let's go down there and find out." Susan headed for the back steps not bothering to lock up the house. With very few neighbors in the area their biggest threat would be a critter coming in the door. Dewey followed as she made her way down the dirt road leading to the far end of the circle where the swinging bridge allowed people to cross the river. Arriving at the bridge before Becky and her male friend, they stood beside what appeared to be Gary's truck, and waited.

"Hi Becky!" Susan greeted her as she descended the steps from the bridge. "Hi Gary! What are ya'll up to?

The surprised look on Becky's face could not hide the guilt she felt at being discovered doing recon. "Oh, we were just hiking." Becky slowed so Gary could catch up with her. She felt the need to ensure Gary kept his mouth shut…or at least agreed with what she said.

Continuing her questioning, "Sure is a strange place to hike. Isn't it difficult?"

"It's more of a challenge," Becky smiled. "What are ya'll doing here?"

Knowing she already knew the answer, Susan played along with the ruse. "We live, or rather I live, down the road in my parents' cabin. Dewey here visits sometimes."

Taking the hint, Dewey jumped into the conversation. "Yeah, I saw someone across from the cabin. First I thought it was animals then realized it was human. Ya'll ok?"

Both Gary and Becky acknowledged they were fine. "Look, we gotta go. We're meeting someone for dinner," Gary continued. "Ya'll have a good evening." With that, Gary hit his key fob unlocking his truck. Becky and Gary entered the truck and drove off, waving at Susan and Dewey.

"Now that was strange," stating the obvious to Susan.

"Ya think?" Susan laughed. Let's go fix some steaks. Heading back up the dirt road and arriving at the cabin, Dewey went to work lighting the grill while Susan poured drinks and prepared the meat for grilling.

~69~

The Federal District Attorney thought Delano had lost his mind requesting search warrants on two different safe deposit boxes; one in Clifton Forge, the other in Roanoke. Arguing his point, Delano was finally successful and had the warrants in hand. First stop was the Blue Ridge Bank in Roanoke since it was closest to his office.

After presenting the warrant to the bank manager, he directed the forensics team to drill the box. Kensie was conspicuously absent from the morning activities. *As much as she has been involved in the investigation, you would have thought she would have wanted to be present for the big reveal. I thought she was too professional to allow her personal feelings to interfere with her job. Guess not.* As Delano waited, he was disappointed with her lack of professionalism. Twenty minutes later, Delano was summoned into the vault. Opening the box, it was empty. "What the hell? It's empty!" He declared to no one in particular. Snapping a photo of the box with his phone he then thanked the bank manager. Heading to Alleghany National Bank with the forensics crew following, he was hoping the results would not be the same.

Calling Kensie, he waited for her to answer, but was greeted with a recording; "You know the drill, name and number. Beep!" Leaving a voice mail, Delano asked her to call him when she got the message.

The one hour drive to Clifton Forge seemed especially long. Having time to think about Kensie, he felt he needed to talk with her about their relationship. Mulling over their last few interactions he could see where she may have misinterpreted his actions. He liked her, but sleeping with her would be like sleeping with his daughter.

Arriving at the bank, he presented the search warrant to the new manager. The forensics team got to work with the same results as in Roanoke. Empty. Completely empty. Perplexed, Delano wondered if the Nicelys were playing games. *I know you've got the money. Now where is it?* Thanking the branch manager, Delano dismissed the forensics team and thanked them for their time and efforts. He then decided to visit the Nicely children. This time he was going to get answers. Come hell or high water.

~70~

The talk around town was that the FBI had drilled Susan Nicely's safe deposit box at the bank only to find it empty. Becky and Gary had finally caught up with Cliff at the tavern. Sitting in a back booth they spoke in whispers in an attempt to prevent anyone nearby from hearing their conversation. Becky had brought proof they were all three siblings. Her print out from the ancestry site showed definitively they were biologically related through their dad. Cliff was speechless. Ordering another beer, he took a long draw from his mug before he could respond.

"How long have you known?" Looking at Becky and Gary.

"We just found out." Becky responded.

Gary confirmed adding, "Yea, I was as shocked as you are. I mean, after all, there are very few secrets in this town, but it looks like this one was the best kept of any."

Cliff agreed. "As small as this town is and as much as people talk, how could our father have three kids by three different women and no one said anything? And we are so close together in age. How was I raised by the man I knew as my dad my entire life and not know he was not my real dad?"

"But he WAS your real dad." Becky pointed out. "Think about it. Who was there to take care of you and provide for you and look out for you?" Cliff didn't answer. He just took another long draw from his beer emptying the mug. He then signaled for the waitress for another.

Once the next beer was delivered, Cliff answered. "Yeah, but think about it. I worked for both of them. They were owners of the construction company. I mean Fitzgerald wasn't around that much…" Cliff took a long drink from his mug. "Maybe he was off getting other women pregnant."

Becky and Gary nodded agreeing with his observation. "It's possible," Gary agreed. "Guess with all these DNA tests out there I'm sure more will probably pop up."

"Did you hear about them drilling the safe deposit boxes at the bank today?" Becky wanted to get to the purpose of the meeting…discreetly.

Snapping back from his thoughts, Cliff said he thought it was just one box. "I thought it was the Nicely box."

Feigning ignorance, Becky said she didn't know whose box it was. "I just heard there were boxes."

"Well, I don't know." Cliff shook his head.

"Why would she have a safe deposit box when she has a vault in her house?" Gary took Becky's lead.

Surprise filled Cliff's face. "She does? I didn't know that."

"Didn't you build the house?" Becky jumped in.

Nodding his head, Cliff confirmed he had built the cabin and also confirmed he had not installed a vault. "Don't know why she would want one. She ain't got no money," he declared.

Buying another round of drinks, Becky decided to order appetizers to thank Cliff for his insight into the house. His confirmation of no vault only meant the money would be easy to find. Seems a break-in is in order.

The stranger sitting at the table closest to the booth strained to listen to the conversation between the new siblings over the din of the crowded tavern. Catching bits and pieces, he was able to learn the relationship was brand new to them and the topic was the stolen money. Observing them, it was clear the woman was in charge. Continuing to listen he learned they believed the money had been moved back to the cabin after making its rounds to several safe deposit boxes in the region. The topic of a vault revealed there was none and a break-in was in order. The stranger knew he would have to beat them to the punch if he wanted his Dad's share of the money. Ordering another beer and dinner, he listened as discreetly as one could in a tavern filling up with locals glad it was the end of the week. The crack of pool balls in the back room followed by cheers or groans also interfered with his ability to hear their plan.

Finishing his dinner, the stranger headed out…destination, the cabin on the Cow Pasture. Recon was in order and he needed to determine the best time to search for the money. Small town talk had disclosed she was a securities attorney working remotely at home. He had also learned that her brother spent a great deal of time with her since the construction had been completed. Neither of which was good news. Learning from his surveillance that the majority of the houses in the area were uninhabited during the week, he figured any time would be a good time since they didn't have neighbors. The timing would depend on their schedule...he could wait...surveil...as long as the time was before the three siblings made their move.

Lights illuminated the interior of the cabin. *One advantage of people believing they are alone, or don't have neighbors, they don't close their curtains or shades...basically living in a fish bowl for all to see.* That attitude served to benefit anyone interested in the habits of their neighbors.

Watching through the binoculars, Susan was walking about the cabin in her lounging pajamas. Carrying a dark red liquid in what appeared to be long stemmed wine glass, she brought a stout glass full of a dark brown liquid to a man sitting on her sofa. *That must be her brother.* Accepting the glass, the male took a sip. The conversation appeared to be relaxed. *Sure wish I'd learned to read lips. What a way to eavesdrop.* The stranger smiled. Continuing to watch, the body language of both the man and the woman, they appeared to be extremely relaxed and enjoying each others company. Eventually, the cabin went dark. The stranger decided to call it a night also deciding to return early the next morning to wait for them to leave.

~71~

Another drive to just east of Clifton Forge brought Delano to the cabin. Having left Roanoke before seven-thirty, he pulled in beside the two vehicles by eight-thirty. *Good morning kids. Time to get serious about what you're hiding.* Knocking on the cabin door, he waited. He knocked again. Again he waited. Hearing the soft padding of muffled foot steps, he waited. Hearing the dead bolt slide, he was soon facing a disheveled male who definitely needed a shave and a strong cup of coffee.

"What do you want?" The greeting was one expected by Delano considering their last meeting.

"I'd like to talk with you and your sister. Is she available?" The door closed in his face. He waited.

A few minutes later, the door was opened by the female resident dressed in blue jeans, sky blue thermal top and thick socks. "Why are you here?" Susan wasn't in any mood to deal with a nosy FBI agent so early in the morning.

Ignoring the attitude, Delano explained he would like to talk with her and her brother about the money taken during the bank robbery fifty years before and the murder of Mr. Clark.

"I thought we made it clear the other day that we had nothing to say to you and we are invoking our right to counsel."

"I understand that, but I don't believe either of you stole the money. Nor do I think you killed Clark."

"I'm listening." Susan stood in the doorway not inviting him in.

"I believe you can help me catch the person who did kill Clark." Susan did not reply. Delano continued. "Look. I have a feeling that your father, the father of Becky Fitzgerald and Johnny Muncy did the armed robbery. But, because they are dead, there isn't a whole lot we can do about it. No one to prosecute."

"Yeah, but I'm betting you would like to recover the money," Susan interrupted.

Confirming her statement, Delano admitted he didn't think the money would ever be recovered, except for the ten grand found at Clark's house. Hoping she would believe his statement about the money, he was also hoping to be invited in. He was.

Ushered into the living room, the house was modestly furnished…as a cabin would be. The contemporary furnishings were in contrast to the rustic feel of the cabin. Sleek, Danish style tables and mission style chairs framed a contemporary sofa. Natural colors of muted oranges, golds, maroons and creams blended the eclectic furnishings.

Directed to a mission style chair, Susan offered Delano a cup of coffee. "Sure, thanks. Black."

Dewey came from the second bedroom now fully awake and dressed. "Why are you here so freaking early man?" Heading to the kitchen he was in search of a cup of very strong coffee. Accepting a cup from Susan he took a seat at one end of the sofa. Susan set Delano's coffee on the end table and assumed a seat at the other end. They waited. Delano took a sip of his coffee.

The stranger sat across the field watching as the suit entered the cabin and then sat opposite the siblings. Facial expressions made it clear the siblings weren't pleased with the early morning visit. *Hell, I wouldn't be either.* All three sipped coffee with the siblings doing more listening than talking. It appeared the suit was pleading a case before a court of law instead of having a general conversation. Standing he began to move toward the window as the female became animated. The other male just sat on the sofa watching his sibling and sipping his coffee. The female stood and moved to the door. As the door opened, it was clear the suit was being asked to leave. Exiting, he stopped and turned to face the female. It was clear from her reaction, she did not like whatever he said. Descending the steps the suit entered his vehicle as the door to the cabin closed. Backing out, the suit turned the vehicle around and headed back to the main road as the stranger watched him pass.

Turning his attention back to the cabin, he watched through the windows as the siblings moved toward the kitchen. Time passed and the stranger was becoming bored when the door opened. The male sibling, carrying what appeared to be an overnight bag, entered his vehicle and headed for the main roadway. *Hum. Maybe he's leaving. Eavesdropping on the conversation of the three siblings at the tavern, they did say he comes and goes for days at a time. Maybe this is a go.* Watching him leave, Dewey never looked to his left noticing the stranger in the car watching and waiting. Not long after, the female exited the cabin. Heading toward the roadway in her MG she too never noticed she was being observed.

After thirty minutes, the stranger approached the cabin on foot. Checking the backdoor, he found it to be locked. Pulling out his pick set he easily entered the home as he pulled on surgical gloves. The layout of the cabin was quite simple. The living room was to the left of the front door with the dining room to the right. The kitchen was separated from the dining room by a short wall and a bathroom sat behind the living room. Starting down the short hallway, there were bedrooms to the right and left; each having its own bath. Sliding glass doors opened from the two bedrooms onto the deck. The hallway went to the back of the cabin between the bedrooms enabling occupants to access the rear deck without passing through either of the bedrooms. Paul entered through the rear door. Sure no one was in the house, he went to what appeared to be the master bedroom. Knowing in his gut the money was somewhere in there, he began to search; first the dresser drawers. Pulling each one out, he checked underneath and behind…nothing. Taking care to return each one to its home, he did his best to leave no indication anyone had been snooping about. He knew that a hundred and forty thousand dollars was a lot of cash so it would take a large amount of space to store it unless it was spread throughout the house. Moving to the closet, he pulled back the clothes to check the wall. It appeared solid. Hearing a noise, he stopped. Unconsciously holding his breath, he sharpened his hearing. Listening. Waiting. *The last thing I need to do is get caught.* No other sound entered his ears. He continued to search. *The money has to be in this house. There is no way she would leave it in her car. That just wasn't secure.* Stopping…he heard another noise…this time from the front of the house. Peaking out the front window, he saw the red MG pulling up to the porch. Hurrying out the backdoor, he made his way down the steps. Trying to conceal his presence behind the pylons, he waited until Susan mounted the stairs to the front deck. Moving to the house to the left of the Nicely house, he kept moving until he reached the tree line. Taking the tree line he walked to the roadway headed for his car.

By the time he cranked the engine, sweat was rolling down his face and his shirt clung to his skin. The air conditioning felt good allowing his body to release its grip on his shirt. *That was close! Wonder if she has the ability to sense that someone was in her cabin? If she does, it's going to make it even more difficult to get back inside and finish the search.* Leaving, Paul headed back to his room at the B&B to grab a shower.

~72~

Cliff was overwhelmed by the news that he had two half siblings. He had left the tavern in a daze. Lots of questions entered his mind as he sat in his living room sipping Jack on the rocks. The single floor lamp cast a spotlight on the chair he sat in and faded to a shadow bringing darkness to his room. Just like the darkness that had been brought to his soul with the revelation of his paternal heritage. *My life was a lie. If Fitzgerald is my biological Dad then who is Burke? How can a man have three kids in a small town like Clifton Forge? Or Covington? Who knew? Am I the laughing stock of this town?* Taking another sip he continued to analyze his life. Suddenly, he realized that Becky and Gary could be part owners in his construction business. He had worked hard most of his life helping the man he thought was his Dad build the business. Every summer he worked long days building homes and making repairs for customers. When his Dad would go out of town, he was running the jobs…assigning workers, handling payroll and soliciting new business. During the school year he somehow managed to attend school, play football and help his Dad run the business. *There is no way I'm letting these two take the business my Dad and I built. I don't care if technically they are my half-siblings. Whose business is it? Fitzgerald's or Burke's? They both worked at it. Fitzgerald owned part because Dad needed financial backing, but he never really did any construction work...at least none that I ever saw.*

"You ok?" The phone had jolted Cliff from his musings. Gary had been concerned when Cliff left abruptly from their meeting.

"Yeah, man. I'm good." Taking another sip from his Jack. "What's up?"

"You mind if I come by?" Thirty minutes later Gary was standing at Cliff's door.

"Come on in, man. You wanna drink?" Cliff ushered Gary into his darkened living room. Moving to turn on a couple more lights, he grabbed another glass from the kitchen. Pouring some brown liquid in the glass he handed it to Gary. "Have a seat man."

Getting to the point, Gary took a sip from his glass. "Look man. I know it's a shock to find out we share the same father. I found out the same way you did...from Becky and that Federal agent.

"What Federal agent?"

The question caught Gary by surprise. "You didn't get interviewed by the Feds?"

"Why would I?" Confused, Cliff had no idea what Gary was talking about. Gary wasn't sure if he should share, but he knew Cliff deserved to know who their Dad was.

"Uh, you might want to bring the bottle into the living room. We need to talk."

Cliff did as suggested. He had a feeling it was going to be a long night...it already had been. *Guess it's gonna be even longer.*

As Gary began the story, he took another sip of the Jack to steel himself. Starting with the bank robbery, Gary disclosed that their father's fingerprints had been found on the money found at Clark's house.

"How did they know it was his?" Pouring more whiskey into both of their glasses, Cliff waited.

Taking another sip of his drink, Gary began. "According to Becky, they got this new technology where they can get fingerprints off of money and then this stuff called touch DNA. You know. The stuff Becky was talking about at the tavern. Cliff admitted that he had glazed over when she started explaining that DNA stuff. "Well, you better pay attention cause it may come back and bite you in the ass if you don't."

Gary continued. "So, the Feds…"

"You going to try to get part of my construction business?" Cliff interrupted.

"What?" The question surprised Gary.

"Are you going to try to get part of my construction business?" Cliff repeated himself.

"I have no interest in your business." Gary stated. "That business is yours. Why would I try to take it from you?"

"Because our Dad and Burke started it," Cliff stated matter-of-factly.

Surprise filled Gary's face. "But, everybody knows you built it."

"That's not an answer." Cliff pointed out.

"I'm not going to try to take your business," Gary stated as he took the bottle and poured more whiskey in their glasses.

"What about Becky?" It was becoming clear to Gary that Cliff was more concerned about losing his business than anything else he had learned today.

Gary stiffened. "All I got to say about Becky is, you better tread lightly. She's focused and will do whatever it takes to get what she wants."

As the hands on the clock moved into the early morning hours, the conversation turned back to the money and the death of Billy. It was clear to Cliff that Gary knew more than what he was sharing. Cliff wasn't sure if Gary was there to check on him and further discuss their relationship or if he was there to gather information for Becky. Cliff's gut was telling him that Gary was Becky's lap dog.

As the sun began to rise over the mountain, Gary stumbled to the door. "Look man. The money taken from the bank is ours. We need to find it. It belonged to our Dad and those other two dads."

"What about Billy?" Cliff asked. Gary did not answer. Stumbling to his truck, he backed out of the driveway and headed home. Cliff hoped he would make it. He couldn't walk so he needed to drive. Closing the door, Cliff laid down on his sofa, passing out.

~73~

Stepping into the cabin, Susan instantly felt the presence of another. With the hairs on the back of her neck standing at attention, she pulled her pepper spray from her handbag. Moving from room to room, she searched for the presence, but found none. Checking her closet, it did not appear that the false wall had been disturbed. *This is not good. My gut has never lied to me. I know someone has been in here. But who? And why?*

Knowing it would be useless to call the police since nothing appeared to be missing and they wouldn't do anything anyway, she called Dewey. "Someone has been in the house."

"What?" The call surprised Dewey. He had returned home so he could keep his job. With a boss losing his patience with frequent absences of his star employee, Dewey wasn't sure how close he was to being let go. "When?"

"After you left this morning I went into town for a while." Susan was still shaken. "When I returned, as soon as I stepped in the door I could feel a presence."

The disclosure did not surprise Dewey. He knew Susan had always had a sixth sense and it served her well. If she said someone had been in the house, then someone had been in the house. Susan had always had dreams that came true and her intuitions were always spot on. "So, you calling the police?" Knowing the answer as soon as he asked, he still waited for her to answer.

"You know I'm not. What are they going to do? Nothing."

"True." Dewey confirmed. "But you should at least file a report so they know it's not the first time when whoever it was comes back."

Thinking for a second, Susan agreed. "I'm going to install cameras around the perimeter that I can access from my phone. If I can see them enter, then maybe, just maybe, I can get the cops out here if whoever was in here comes back."

Liking her decision, Dewey pointed out that the Alleghany County Sheriff's Office was spread pretty thin with the amount of land they have to patrol. "The chances of them getting there to catch whoever it is is pretty slim. Why don't you set a trap?"

"That's a thought. But I don't know what type of trap."

"Do you know how they got in?"

"I don't."

Thinking for a minute, Dewey suggested that they had to have picked the lock if there is no sign of forced entry. "If that's the case, you're dealing with a pro. Let me think on that and I'll give you a call back."

"OK." Susan agreed.

"Just keep your gun close. If they didn't take anything then they didn't find what they were looking for. That means they'll be back." The statement did not give Susan a good feeling at all.

"Thanks. Like I needed to hear that."

"Hey. Just being honest. You know I can't come back right now. I need to work. Boss is getting irritated with me taking so much time off with short notice. I'll be back in a couple weeks for the long week-end."

"No. I'll be fine." She lied. "Why don't you come back when I get the security system and help me install the cameras. If I order them today they'll be here by the time you return." With the plan in place, Dewey disconnected the call. Concerned filled his mind, but he knew his little sister could handle whatever came her way.

With the report filed, Susan grabbed her laptop and began researching security cameras. Deciding on a configuration that gave her eight cameras and two Ring doorbells, she knew they would arrive by the time Dewey returned. In the meantime, she would stay close to home to ensure whoever had been in her house wasn't able to return until the cameras were installed. Calling Cliff, she had him send an electrician out to install a couple of WiFi security lights further out toward the river.

~74~

With her security shaken by the break-in, Susan was unable to sleep as soundly as she had before. Every little noise would wake her and when she went to the river she would carry her keys ensuring that the doors were locked. The only windows left open were on the sides where no porches were. *They'll have to bring a ladder if they want in that way or rappel down from the roof.* Sitting on the shore, the water was still too cold for wading or swimming. She sat facing up river so she would watch both the water and the house. *Oh, I don't like feeling like this. Whoever stole my security needs to pay. But who could it be? Who would have an interest in what was inside?*

Reviewing the activities of the past few months, somehow she knew it was tied to the money. *Becky could be a suspect. It's strange that she was in Richmond at the library the same time as me and Dewey. She said she was doing topography research on some land, but she was probably researching the money like we were. But, did she know how to pick locks? I doubt it. That agent said there were three robbers; Daddy, Becky's dad and another guy named Muncy. Wonder who that Muncy person was? Wonder if they have any kids around here. Who would know?* Heading toward the cabin, she decided to get a glass of wine. *It's always five o'clock somewhere.*

Susan watched Becky's dark blue Mazda come down the

hill and drive past the church leaving a dusty cloud in her wake. Pulling up beside Susan's MG, Becky took her time exiting her car. "What happened to your car, Becky?" A look of confusion filled Becky's face. "Your bumper and right fender...did someone hit you?"

Looking back at her car, Becky replied, "Oh. That. Uh, someone backed into me. Insurance is delaying the repairs."

"Don't you just hate that? If their insured is at fault they should just pay." Becky agreed. "Come on up. Would you like some wine?"

"Sure." Becky mounted the steps to the front deck. "Wow! This place has really changed. I heard you had it completely rebuilt."

"I did. Would you like a tour?" Entering the house before Becky, Susan turned to watch her reaction. "I don't think you've ever been inside have you?" Hesitating, Becky confirmed Susan's statement. Making her way to the kitchen, Susan grabbed a wine glass and poured chardonnay for Becky and topped hers off. Once the tour was finished, Becky was invited to sit on the back deck. "It's so much nicer hearing the river."

Conversation covered such topics as the demolition and reconstruction of the cabin, old times in high school and the progress of Clifton Forge coming back from the brink of extinction. "I'm really proud of our little town," Susan declared. Becky agreed.

After several glasses of wine, Susan revealed the fact of the break-in. The response of Becky appeared one of complete and authentic surprise. If she was faking her response, it was difficult to say. "Did they get anything?" Shaking her head, Susan shared they had not. "I just know you must be shaken."

"Yes, I am. But Dewey is coming back soon. All will be fine." Changing the subject, Susan wanted to get to the true reason for inviting Becky to visit…other than to see her reaction to the break-in. "Do you remember a family named Muncy?"

A fleeting look of confusion crossed Becky's face, but was quickly replaced with one of recollection. "Oh, you mean the Muncy mentioned in the article about the robbery?" She left out the fact that both of their fathers were mentioned in the same article.

"Yes. What was his first name? Jeff? Jay?"

"I believe it was Johnny."

"Oh, yes. Johnny. Did you know anything about that family?"

Shaking her head, "No. I don't. And I've asked around and no one seems to remember that family. Isn't that just sad?" As the discussion progressed, both agreed it was sad the number of families that just seemed to disappear from memory. "Maybe they moved east like a lot of the families did. You know…with the railroad. A lot of families went to the Newport News area because of the railroad. Some left when they joined the military and never returned."

Agreeing with all Becky said Susan nodded. "Yes, or went away to college and never returned. Someone must remember them."

"Well, it would have to be one of the Old Timers left in town. You know they still meet at the Bull Pen for breakfast every morning. And when I say breakfast, I mean they are there around seven in the morning."

Surprised, "Well, I guess the more things change, the more they stay the same." Susan laughed.

"Look. I gotta be going." Becky stood to leave. "Your place is really nice. It was good reminiscing and thanks for the wine." Descending the back stairs, Becky headed for her car. Susan watched until she was out of sight. Moving to the front porch, Susan discretely photographed the car before Becky drove away. Watching her drive by the church, Becky disappeared into a cloud of dust finally reappearing at the top of the hill and heading into town.

~75~

The next morning, Susan found herself at the Bull Pen. Memories came flooding back as she remembered the days her father would bring her with him for breakfast. Recognizing a couple of the Old Timers, she walked over and introduced herself. As soon as their memories allowed them to remember her, she was hugged so tightly she could barely breathe followed by being held by both arms and thrust backward so they could "take a look at her." Asked to sit at the main table, it was clear to the stranger, who sat at one of the side tables, that Susan was definitely remembered and well liked. Sentences such as "I haven't seen you since you were this high" while holding their hand down about waist high to show how short she was. Or, "I haven't seen you since you were knee high to a coke bottle." Laughter always followed and a kiss on the cheek was planted by many of the much older men. As the biscuits, gravy, ham and eggs were delivered plate by plate, conversation flowed. Stories were told hand in hand with tall tales. Susan laughed so hard her face was hurting.

"So, to what do we owe the honor of your presence, Miss Susan? We know you been in town for a while, but you haven't bothered to come see us." Pat Patterson pointed out.

"We also hear from Cliff you tore down the old home place and built a spanking new house in the same spot."

"Did you raise it up some?" Junior Buzzard asked. "I hope you did 'cause if you didn't you gonna get wet when the rains come." The laughter roared with his declaration.

Laughing Susan confirmed the house had been raised and she should be fine when the rains came. "The only thing I'll have to worry about is my car."

"Ah hell Susan." Junior laughed. "That ain't no big deal. We can get you a real car. Not that little go cart you're running around in." The laughter roared again. Susan couldn't help but laugh.

Attempting to change the subject Susan asked if anyone remembered the Muncy family. "Muncy family?" Patterson questioned. "Didn't he do that bank robbery?" Silence fell over the crowd. Patterson had tread into a subject the other's believed would be touchy. The stranger perked up. The Old Timers had finally been presented a topic he was most interested in. Waiting for someone to answer, he knew he would be sticking around the Bull Pen for a little longer today.

Susan broke the silence. "It's ok guys. I know my Dad was one of the suspects." There was a collective sigh of relief as she made her announcement. "I've read the newspapers and I also know he wasn't the only suspect. I read there were three of them. My Dad, Becky Fitzgerald's dad and a guy named Johnny Muncy." Heads nodded. "If he did do the robbery, he sure didn't share the take." Susan's statement brought laughter from the Old Timers. The stranger didn't laugh. He just focused.

Junior spoke first. "Hey Monroe. Didn't you live next door to the Muncys?"

"I did…when I was a teenager. But, they moved before the robbery. That's why it was surprising he was named as one of the three." Monroe confirmed.

"Where'd they move?" Susan asked.

"Gosh. Uh…let me think." It looked like he went inside his memory trying to recover information filed away from fifty years before. "You know," Monroe began, "I may have killed off those brain cells." Laughter erupted again.

"Well, if you'd stayed away from that shine, you might still have some brain cells left." Persinger stated the obvious.

The look of revelation filled Monroe's face. "They went east. I think." Putting his hand to his chin to rub his whiskers, "I think old man Muncy went to work at the shipyard in Newport News." Thinking a little more he confirmed his declaration. "Yep. He went to the shipyard."

Buzzard interjected. "I think he went down there 'cause he kept gettin' laid off from the railroad. Every time John L. Lewis would call a strike, he was first to be let go." The mere mention of Lewis' name was like throwing cold water on a hot fire. "That man brought hardship on everyone connected to the coal miners and the businesses affected by them…especially us railroaders." All the others agreed by either nodding or adding an amen.

"Did he have any kids?" Susan was glad the Muncys were remembered; at least by a couple of the Old Timers. It was clear her next question wasn't as easily answered. Shaking their heads, no one could say for sure.

"But I'm sure they did. We all had kids. That's just what you did when you got married." All the men nodded.

The stranger spoke up. "They had kids." The revelation brought silence to the room and every eye was on him. "I'm Johnny's son." If the room was silent before, it became even more silent, if that was even possible. The only noise penetrating the room was the screeching of the rail cars coming to a stop and the banging and clanging of the cars as they coupled. It was as if no one dared to breathe. This stranger who had been sitting amongst them for weeks was the son of the third suspected bank robber.

Susan was the first to break the silence. "So, how long have you been in town?"

"Long enough." The stranger responded.

"And how long is that?" Susan pressed.

Junior Buzzard answered for him, "He's been here a couple months 'cause he's been here with us just about every morning." Anger began to rise in his voice. "So, why you here? You spyin' on us?" A chorus of "yeahs" followed Buzzard's question.

Attempting to calm the group of men, he shared he was born in Hampton, but he knew his parents were from Clifton Forge. Disclosing he had found a diary of his mother's that talked of his father disappearing occasionally, he was in search of learning where his father would go. "Sitting here listening to ya'll talking made me feel closer to my Dad. He wasn't around much and now I think I know why."

Susan wasn't buying his explanation and she knew neither were the Old Timers. Knowing she needed to talk to him alone, she also needed to get him out of the Bull Pen before he was lynched. "Hey guys?" Susan turned to the Old Timers. "Let me talk to this guy." Her look toward Monroe was one of "help me calm these guys." Message received.

Monroe jumped in. "Hey, let's let Susan talk to this guy and see what he's up to." Eventually they agreed allowing Susan and the stranger to leave.

~76~

Walking down Ridgeway Street, Susan suggested they go to the library where they could get a private study room and talk without interruption. Securing the room, Susan arranged to sit facing the door and the stranger facing her. Turning on the voice recorder on her phone without the stranger's knowledge, she kept her phone in her lap. "First off, what is your name?

"Paul Muncy." The reaction on Susan's face spoke volumes. "I'm John Paul Muncy, Jr." He smiled. "People call me Paul."

"So, Paul Muncy. The Old Timers say you've been in town for at least a couple of months and you say you've been here because of your Mom's diary."

"Yea. So?" Paul was not going to become forthcoming with any information. He knew she had the money from the robbery in her house and he intended to get it. He smiled to himself. *You have no idea I've been in your house.*

Susan tried to hide that she had assumed the attorney attitude. She also turned on her internal lie detector. "So this is a very small town with not much happening. Why have you been here for a couple of months?"

"Just looking around. Thinking about moving here."

"Why? Rarely does anyone move here unless they have family here," observed Susan.

"Well, I had family here. You moved here from Northern Virginia." The response surprised Susan. A surprise Susan had difficulty hiding. He smiled to himself.

"How do you know that?"

A smug smile crossed Paul's face. "Where you've been all these years is not one of the secrets they kept."

After an hour of back and forth, it was clear Susan was going to get nowhere with this John Paul Muncy, Jr. Her instincts told her there was more to the story than what he was sharing. She would be visiting the Old Timers in the morning to give them a heads up on this stranger. "Well, thanks for talking to me. I hope you find what you're looking for. Seems our Dads may have known each other back in the day. But, no offense, we can just know of each other."

"No problem. Take care of yourself." With that, John Paul Muncy, Jr. stood, offered his hand to Susan to shake. Susan declined. Withdrawing his hand he turned and left the library.

Shutting off the recorder, Susan walked back to the Bull Pen to find it empty of any Old Timers. *Just as I suspected. They'll be here in the morning I know. I'll see them then.*

~77~

The red pick-up truck rested nose down in the Cow Pasture River off of route forty-two just south of Carter's Place. The impact of the crash into the guard rail and then down the embankment was sufficient enough to deploy the airbags thrusting the head of the driver against the back window of the cab. Being knocked unconscious, the driver's head was submerged under the water as he fell to the right, lying on the seat. It didn't help that he had been drinking Jack Daniels on the rocks all night with nothing on his stomach.

Spotted by a passing truck, the State Police responded long before the sheriff's deputy arrived. Observing damage to the left rear bumper, it appeared the truck was struck from behind being forced from the roadway. Barely striking the guardrail the truck traveled another fifty feet before it came to a stop with the front wheels, hood and part of the cab submerged in the moving water. Papers floated around the cab of the truck, an indication of the jobs lined up for the now deceased truck occupant. A pair of brown canvas gloves rested on the dashboard, not yet touched by the flowing water.

Snapping photos of the crash scene, the trooper advised the deputy he would handle the investigation since the sheriff's office was undermanned. The news did not bother the deputy at all. He hated working crashes and didn't care to work a fatality. The deputy did offer to assist with the dummy end of the tape measure as the trooper took measurements of the tire marks and distance traveled. Once the wrecker arrived, the pick-up was pulled from the river. The body was removed from the cab and transported to the medical examiner's office in Roanoke.

Inspecting the rear section of the truck, Trooper Jackson found dark blue paint on the left rear bumper as well as the left side of the truck bed. Grabbing an evidence envelope and his knife he scraped the paint into the envelope, sealing it and noting the date and time on the seal. Additional photos of the truck were taken before the wrecker towed it to the State Forensics garage in Roanoke where the forensics investigators would go over it with a fine tooth comb. Ensuring the cab was locked and the keys were sealed in another envelope, Trooper Jackson allowed the wrecker driver to head to Roanoke.

~78~

Delano was at his desk when Alice called to let him know she had something of interest in the morgue. Just as he hung up from her call, Kensie called to let him know he needed to come down to the forensics garage. "I have something that just might interest you." Unsure which was more important, Delano chose the morgue which meant a body.

"Agent Delano, meet Gary Fitzgerald." The introduction surprised Delano.

"What happened?" Delano observed the body laid out on the slab. He appeared to have been dead for a while and his skin was pruny.

"Traffic crash. Seems he missed the bridge and hit the river. Looks like he drowned, but I'll know more once I finish the autopsy."

"Anything else?"

"He has a gash in the back of his head. I'm betting it will show his head busted the back window. The truck is over in the forensics garage."

"That must be what Kensie wants me to come see."

A little jealousy filled Alice, but she remained professional. "As you can see there was some bruising on his face so I doubt he was wearing his seatbelt. He was in the water a while because his skin is pruny. You know, like when you lay in the tub too long?" Alice smiled.

Delano grinned. "I haven't laid in a tub too long in a very, very long time. Anything else?"

"Nope. I'll give you a call when I finish. I'll pull his blood to see if he was sober when he crashed. Now, go see your girl Kensie." Alice grinned, but Delano could feel the ice in the comment.

Heading down the long tiled hallway, he turned left at the corner and headed for the garage in a detached building. Walking through the door he found Kensie in her coveralls...a completely different look from her usual office attire. *I think I prefer the Boho look.* With her hair pinned up, she looked more mature than her thirty-five years. "Hi Kensie. You summoned?"

The chill still wasn't gone. "Where you been?"

"I stopped by the morgue. Evidently the body that belongs to the truck is laying over there." It was clear she did not like his response.

"Well then, as you already know, I got Gary Fitzgerald's truck. Seems he decided to go off roading and ended up in the river. From what I can tell so far, the truck was submerged for quite a while. The airbags deployed and there is a spider web crack in the back window...probably caused by him hitting his head on the window. There is some dark blue paint on some damage to the left rear bumper and I found more dark blue paint on the left side of the truck bed just in front of the bumper. You need to find a car with dark blue paint and some damage to the right front bumper." Kensie was very matter-of-fact.

"Have you inventoried the contents of the truck?"

"Yep. Just some papers and a pair of brown canvas gloves?" That answer piqued Delano's interest.

"Where are the gloves?"

Walking toward a stainless steel table beside the truck, Kensie picked up a paper bag that had been sealed with red and white tape, initials and a date written across the tape. "Here they are."

"Mind if I open the bag?"

Kensie shrugged. "It's your case. Do whatever you want."

Taking the bag, Delano cut the seal removing the gloves that were still slightly damp from being lapped with water. Examining the gloves, he noticed a tear in the right glove. "I'm going to take these over to Alice. I think she's got something that may match."

"That's fine. It's your chain of evidence. Do what you want." It wasn't getting any warmer in the garage. It seemed to Delano that the mention of Alice's name brought the temperature down several degrees. *At this rate I'll have frost bite before I even leave the garage...and it's Summer!* Heading for the door, Delano asked Kensie to keep him posted. Kensie didn't answer.

Halfway up the hallway, Delano ran into Trooper Jackson. Shaking hands, Delano explained that the driver was a suspect in one of his investigations and he had taken a pair of gloves found in the cab of the truck. "You wanna take over the investigation?" The trooper asked.

"Nah. I got enough on my plate. Why don't we work it together?" Delano suggested.

"Works for me." Jackson agreed.

Nodding, Delano said he would text him when he's finished with Alice. "We can sit down and I can bring you up to speed."

"Sounds good."

~79~

Delivering the gloves to Alice, Delano announced he believed he had found the owner of the glove piece found in Clark's teeth. This revelation surprised Alice. Never thinking a match would be found, she had not given it a second thought. "OK. Well, I'll get the piece to Kensie along with the glove and have her test to make sure they are the same. "Were the gloves submerged?"

"Not completely, but they did get a little wet."

Taking the bag containing the gloves from Delano, Alice initialed and dated it under his. "OK. Well. I'll keep you posted on what we find."

Heading to his office, Delano texted the trooper letting him know he was ready to meet. Thirty minutes later, they were sitting across from each other at the coffee shop across the street from the Federal Building.

"So, what's the story on this Gary Fitzgerald?" Trooper Jackson started.

"I believe he was murdered." Delano was matter-of-fact in his statement.

The disclosure surprised Jackson. "And why do you think that?" For the next hour Jackson listened as Delano started from the beginning. First the bank robbery from fifty years before, then the missing money from the safe deposit box and then found at the bank manager's house and the bank manager being found dead. As Delano talked, Jackson could not believe what he was hearing. He had been in law enforcement for more than seventeen years and had never run across the likes of this case. Delano continued to talk about the fingerprints found on the money and the touch DNA. He explained how Gary was connected to the story by way of being half-blood related to a woman named Becky and a man named Cliff. Their father was suspected of being one of the original bank robbers.

Continuing, he spoke of Susan and his belief that she had the remaining hundred and forty thousand dollars, but he had no way to prove it. He also talked about the death of Clark and the brown canvas found between Clark's teeth. "I believe the canvas gloves found in Fitzgerald's truck will match the canvas found between Clark's teeth. I don't think Fitzgerald meant to kill Clark. According to the ME he died from the trauma to the back of his head...of course, his cheek bone was smashed in and he had a broken eye socket, but I don't think that killed him.

Taking a sip of his coffee, Delano looked at the trooper. "I'm gonna need your help on this." The trooper nodded. "I've never done accident reconstruction and I'm going to need you to do that for me.

"I'll do whatever I can to help. I need to find the dark blue vehicle to match the paint I took from the truck."

"That should be fairly easy since people like to talk. You got my cell. I got yours. Let's get this person who killed Fitzgerald. I'm sure they are connected to Clark's death and I know they are connected to the money." Jackson nodded. Calling for the check, both law enforcement officers returned to their respective offices; Delano's brick and mortar, Jackson's sheet metal, rubber and cloth…aka his patrol unit.

~80~

News of Gary's death rocked the community. A guy that everyone liked and someone who would go out of his way to help people will be greatly missed. Talk around town was that he had been murdered. In a community where murders just didn't happen caused the locals to be on alert and more suspicious of strangers. They usually rolled up the sidewalks around night fall, but it was clear people were staying closer to home and, when going out, never went out alone. People were scared. The tavern was empty and the other shops on Ridgeway were losing business since Gary's demise. People were demanding answers from the police chief. He had none.

Everyone knew Gary had no family left so the local funeral home stepped up to take possession of Gary's remains once the Medical Examiner had finished with them. One of the older citizens donated an extra plot he owned at Mountain View Cemetery and the florist donated the flowers for his casket. Standing room only was the case in the chapel of the funeral home the day of the funeral. Many good words were spoken about Gary's love of life, love of friends and his willingness to help people out. Some said he wouldn't hurt a fly.

Delano, sitting in the back of the funeral home knew better. The results of the forensics tests on the gloves had come back. The piece of canvas found between Clark's teeth matched the canvas on the work gloves found in Gary's truck. But the question he needed to answer now was; with all these people thinking so highly of Gary Fitzgerald, who would want him dead? Surveying the crowd, he noticed Becky standing on one side of the chapel and Susan with Dewey across from her; neither appeared to be particularly grieved by Gary's demise.

As the service paused, the preacher invited those in attendance to come to the cemetery for the conclusion. Mourners filed out of the chapel, greeting each other with handshakes or hugs. Delano watched as Susan, Dewey and Becky filed out. They were soon joined by Cliff Burke appearing particularly shaken. Susan gave him a hug, Dewey a handshake. Becky tried to slip past him, unsuccessfully. Grabbing her wrist, she quickly turned to face him trying to withdraw her arm…unsuccessfully.

"Can we talk?" It sounded like a question, but the look on his face told Becky it was a command.

"Now? This is not a good time." Pulling her arm away, Cliff released her.

Blocking her way to the vehicles, Cliff advised her that now was an excellent time. "Why don't you ride with me? We can talk on the way to the cemetery."

Looking around, this was definitely not what Becky wanted. She knew Gary had spent the night before his death at Cliff's. Having snuck around the house, she had managed to peep in a couple of the windows watching them sipping Jack Daniels and having what appeared to be, a very serious discussion. At one point, Gary had stood before Cliff pacing back and forth as if his life depended on what he was saying. Whatever the topic of discussion was, Becky knew it wasn't good. Her gut had told her Gary was telling Cliff all about the money and his assignment to find the missing ten thousand dollars. Her observations through the window were what had prompted her to wait down the road for Gary to leave, following him home and then helping him drive into the Cow Pasture. "Look. Can we talk later?"

"No, we need to talk now." Taking Becky by the arm, Cliff escorted her to his truck helping her inside. Turning left on Ridgeway Street to follow the procession to the cemetery, the discussion between them became very heated. Soon they were yelling at each other...Cliff in an accusatory voice, knew Becky had something to do with Gary's demise; Becky deny everything. Continuing the argument as they parked, their voices could be heard by the mourners walking past Cliff's truck. Delano, Susan and Dewey watched from afar.

Volunteering to bring up the rear of the procession to the cemetery gave Trooper Jackson an opportunity to inspect the assorted vehicles parked around the funeral home. None appeared to have any damage that would have matched the damage on the rear of Gary's truck. Once all occupied vehicles had departed, only one remained…a rental. Jackson found this odd and reported his observation to Delano who was in the procession.

Noting the license plate, Jackson followed the procession while calling into communications to run the plate. Coming back to a car repair shop in Lewisburg, West Virginia, Jackson advised Delano asking him to contact Kensie to determine when the car was rented.

Delano did as requested and found the car to have been rented to one Becky Fitzgerald the day before the funeral. "It appears that her car is having some body work done and she will need the rental for at least a week."

Upon hearing that, Jackson headed for Lewisburg. Forty-five minutes later he pulled into the lot of Bubba's Car Repair. Knowing he was not going to be the most popular person who had entered the establishment, Jackson took care to note the locations of the assorted employees. "Is Bubba here?"

A large burly toothless wonder covered in tattoos blocked his entrance into the office, "Who wants to know?"

"You wanna go to jail for obstruction?" Jackson was not in the mood to play games with some grease monkey. "Where's Bubba?"

Standing to the side allowing Jackson to enter, he found Bubba sitting behind the counter talking on the phone and pushing keys on the computer keyboard. Jackson waited.

"Little out of your jurisdiction aren't you trooper?" Bubba grinned as he hung up the phone. Extending his hand, he shook Jackson's and pulled him in for a hug.

"Just a little." Jackson grinned. "How you been man? How's business?"

Bubba grinned. "Good. Good. When you hanging it up man? I could use a partner." Bubba had been a West Virginia State Trooper for twenty-five years. Retiring on disability, he took over his Dad's auto body shop three years before making it one of the premier shops in the region. People came from all over to have his guys repair their cars. Everyone knew when the car left his shop it would be right and the paint always matched.

"I still got a few years, man. I'm working a case that you can help me with. Seems you rented a car to a woman. I'm hoping you have her car here and you haven't started repairs."

Moving back to his computer, Bubba rested his fingers on the keys, fire away, man."

"Becky Fitzgerald, you rented…"

Bubba interrupted Jackson. "A mint green Mazda. Yeah, she came in yesterday. Brought in her dark blue Mazda. Said someone ran into her car at the store. You wanna see it?" Moving toward the door leading to the shop, Jackson followed. "Looks more like she hit someone than the other way around," Bubba grinned. "You can take the guy outta law enforcement, but you can't take the law enforcement outta the guy."

"I hope you haven't started on it."

Shaking his head, "Nah, we're pretty backed up. It's gonna be a few days." Walking through a bay containing a Porsche, Bubba continued to the back of the garage. "We got a couple ahead of her. Told her that when she came in." Motioning to the dark blue Mazda with damage to the front right fender and a bumper pushed back into the wheel well, Jackson was surprised it was drivable.

"How in the world did she drive it in? Isn't the wheel well hitting the tire?" Jackson moved closer to inspect the damage.

"Nah. She must have had someone pull it away from the tire. Either that or she missed it by about a half inch. Not much clearance."

"Ok. Uh, let's go back to the office. We need to talk."

"Sure." Closing the door to the office, no ears could hear their conversation. Jackson began from the beginning disclosing almost everything Delano had disclosed a few days earlier. He shared the information about the fatality pointing out that based on the information learned from Delano and the connection between the owner of the car Bubba had in his shop and the victim of the fatality, Jackson believed that car was the car that forced Gary off the road and into his grave.

"I need to get a search warrant and take the car back to Roanoke. Who's working this area right now?"

"Probably Fisher. He's been on for about ten years. He's good. You want me to call?"

Jackson nodded. "Yea. See if he's tied up. I'm gonna need a West Virginia search warrant and I need it to stand up to scrutiny."

"Well, he's the one you need." Picking up the phone, Bubba was able to dial the number by heart. Turning to grin at Jackson as he waited for an answer on the other line; "Kinda like your academy weapon serial number, the number is ingrained." Jackson laughed. "Hey, it's Knoaker." Bubba spoke into the receiver. "Fisher working?" He listened. "I need him to respond here." He listened again. "Ok. Thanks." Hanging up the phone; "He's on his way." As they waited, lies were swapped and the bull was shot.

Twenty minutes later a mountain of a man entered the office. Standing a good six foot five and tipping the scale at about two fifty, Fisher was the size of man you needed working this area of West Virginia; an area where people could disappear without a trace. The majority of people were related and no one ever knew anything about anything. As a law enforcement officer, if you couldn't hold your own with a crowd of suspects wanting to see you disappear, you'd never solve any crimes and no one would ever trust you. Fisher had been successful developing relationships with those who lived back in the hollars. Because of that, word had spread through the community that he was a straight shooter. If he jammed you up, you were definitely guilty. The high and tight red hair and freckles across the bridge of his nose made him look like a young kid; a definite contradiction to his stature and the reputation he carried daily.

Introductions were made and Fisher was brought up to speed about the case being worked by Jackson. Jackson advised him that he would need Fisher to obtain a search warrant for the car sitting in the back of Bubba's shop. Asking questions, Fisher needed clarification before he would agree to obtain the warrant. Once all of his questions were answered, he agreed to help with the investigation…especially since Bubba vouched for Jackson.

~81~

Watching Susan and Dewey enter the funeral home, Muncy headed toward the cabin. He knew he had at least an hour before they would return. He needed to get inside and search the house again. Picking the backdoor lock, he entered, setting off the motion sensors installed the week before. Susan's phone vibrated as she watched Becky and Cliff argue in his truck. Opening the app she watched the face that had been sitting across from her at the library walking toward the camera. Nudging Dewey, she held the phone so he could see the screen. "Look."

"Who is that?" Dewey had no idea.

Starting for her car, she grabbed Dewey's sleeve to have him follow. "That, dear brother, is John Paul Muncy, Jr. Taking the driver's seat and weaving backwards through the parked cars, she passed Cliff's truck. Finally reaching the corner, Susan turned the car around and floored the accelerator speeding along the tree line, past the mausoleum recessed into the side of the hill. Reaching the entrance of the cemetery, the MG rocketed eastbound onto Main Street heading toward the cabin. Dewey watched Muncy on Susan's phone as they sped onto the interstate reaching route forty two within minutes. Exiting the interstate, Susan swung the car northbound sliding on loose gravel. "Whoa Mutt! Don't kill us!" Susan didn't respond.

Suddenly, a sheriff's deputy appeared behind them. Susan accelerated completely ignoring the lights and siren. Speeding toward the bridge, she barely slowed almost launching them onto the railroad tracks below after striking the cement barrier. She continued to accelerate winding her way up the hill and through the curves to the right and left. Dewey was hanging on with one hand while watching the man moving through his sister's cabin. Slowing to make the turn at the church, the deputy was close behind almost overshooting the turn. Flying past the church, Susan slammed on brakes as she reached the cabin, jumping from the car and running toward the back. Dewey followed…so did the deputy.

The noise of Susan's and Dewey's approach, followed by the sirens, had alerted Muncy. Looking out the front window, he ran for the backdoor reaching it just as Susan bailed from her car. Jumping the railing, Muncy landed hard falling forward on his knees. Susan ran directly toward him covering the ground under the house. Jumping on his back, she wrapped her arms around his neck…her weight keeping him on the ground.

Dewey and the deputy joined her. They were soon joined by another deputy and a trooper who had heard the pursuit over the radio.

Pulling Susan from Muncy's back, the deputy took control of him as Susan yelled obscenities and accusations. Dewey took control of Susan trying to calm her down. Pacing back and forth and taking deep breaths, she was finally able to gain control. In doing so, she was able to explain to the first deputy what had happened. Directing Dewey to retrieve her phone from the car, she showed the deputy the security footage. Seeing that, Muncy was placed under arrest. "I'm going to need you to file an official report." Nodding, Susan agreed.

"Do I need to come to headquarters?"

"If you could." The deputy confirmed. "And we can talk about your driving." The deputy grinned.

~82~

With the affidavit filled out, Jackson and Fisher went to see the judge. After several questions were answered, the two troopers left with the search warrant in hand. Returning to Bubba's, Fisher served the warrant on Bubba who placed it in his legal file.

With a couple of small manila envelopes, a sharp knife and camera in hand, Jackson headed back to the suspect vehicle. Snapping several photos, he then took paint samples from the damaged area. Noticing a small amount of red paint on the bumper, Jackson also scraped it into another envelope. With both envelopes sealed, dated and initialed he then asked Bubba if there was a wrecker available to tow the car to Roanoke. There was. Having sealed the doors with evidence tape, the car was loaded ready for the two hour trip to the FBI lab in Roanoke.

Turning to Fisher, "You'll be filing the executed warrant with the courts?"

"I will." Fisher confirmed. "I'll send you a copy as soon as it's filed. You got an address?"

Handing Fisher his card, the two troopers said their goodbyes. Thanking Bubba for his help, Jackson headed east to Roanoke following the flatbed wrecker.

~83~

Once again, shocking headlines covered the top of the local newspaper lying on the table at the Bull Pen. "I knew that guy was no good," Junior Buzzard declared. "You could see it in his eyes. Always sitting to the side just listening."

"Yea, can you believe he broke into Susan's house?" Patterson asked. "Anybody know how she's doing?" No one answered. Some shook their heads.

"Anybody know what he was looking for?" Junior asked. Again, no one could answer. "Well, she's one feisty girl. Glad she caught him. I hear she jumped him and held him down till the deputy got there."

"Hell, I hear the deputy was chasing her 'cause she was driving so fast." Laughter roared through the Bull Pen as the door opened and Susan entered followed by Dewey. "Well, well, well," Junior began, "Here's Speedy Gonzales and her sidekick Slowpoke Rodriquez now." Once again the laughter roared. "Come on in Speedy." Pulling out a chair for Susan to join him at his table, he patted the seat. "Come tell us about your life of crime." Susan laughed taking the seat Junior had pulled out. The waitress brought her a cup of black coffee and a word of warning…" Watch these guys darlin' they are wound up today," then winked.

Dewey took a chair at another table and was also served coffee. "You want anything to eat darlin'?" Karen licked the tip of her pencil prepared to take his order.

"No. I'm good for now. But Speedy might be hungry. You know its hard work running from the cops and tackling crooks." He laughed. Susan gave him a look that screamed "don't encourage them".

"Ok. Speedy." Patterson held up the morning paper so everyone could read the large, bold headlines. "Give us the low down." Susan laughed and took another sip of her coffee.

"Yeah. Spill." Buzzard commanded and the others agreed nodding their heads or declaring "yeah".

Sitting up in her chair ensuring she could see everyone, she began the story starting with the first break-in…leaving out the part about the money. Disclosing she had installed cameras in the house, she shared that she had received an alert at Gary's funeral and saw Muncy snooping through her house. "I wasn't about to let him get away with it again. That's why I took off." The crowd laughed.

"So, how'd the cops get there so quick?" Buzzard asked the burning question.

Susan blushed. "Uh, well, uh, I was going a little faster than the speed limit."

Shifting in his seat, Dewey blurted out, "Now THAT'S an understatement. She was flying." He laughed. So did the crowd at the Bull Pen. Dewey continued. "She flew off the interstate sliding sideways. Must have been a deputy sitting up at The Triangle or something, but he was on her." Laughter filled the room and all the men were giving high fives to each other, Susan and Dewey. "I thought we were going off the bridge at the tracks." Dewey declared. "But she didn't even slow down. The deputy didn't catch up until she slowed to make the turn at the church." The laughter became so loud they could barely hear Dewey talk and several men were grabbing their sides. "I thought we were goin' flyin' off the cliff."

"An-ee-way!" Susan interrupted. "We caught the guy and he's in jail for breaking into my house." Heads nodded and high fives were all around again.

As the clock hands moved toward noon, the topics of conversation changed like the wind. The most somber of topics was the deaths of Billy and Gary. Neither had been solved and no one knew of any news.

Knowing the deaths had to be connected to the money, Susan and Dewey became a little tense when that topic was raised. "I'm sure they'll solve them soon." Standing, Susan declared they must be going. Dewey stood to leave.

Junior stood to give Susan a hug. "Well, we're all glad you're ok. Now, let's see if you can do the speed limit…or at least close to it from now on." Agreeing to try Susan laughed and returned the hug. "Ya'll take care."

~84~

Sharing a cup of coffee at the shop across from FBI headquarters, Jackson and Delano were taking a break from their hectic lives since joining forces. The car had arrived at Kensie's garage where she had gone over it with a fine tooth comb. Running prints she was able to lift from the interior she found prints belonging to Becky and Bubba from the body shop and Clark. She called Delano to share the news.

"Clark?" That disclosure surprised Delano. "You sure?"

"Yes, I'm sure." The frost was still in her voice, but he could detect a slight thaw.

"Where on the car were Clark's prints?"

"The passenger door. Only got a couple of partials but they were enough for a match. So, your first dead guy was in her car."

"Ok. Thanks Kensie. I'll talk with you soon." Disconnecting the call, Delano shared the news with Jackson. "Well, it appears your suspect had my dead guy in her car."

"Well, didn't you say the money connected all of them?" Delano nodded his head. "So, they could have been friends." Jackson observed. "After all, Clifton Forge is a small town. Everybody knows everybody." Delano agreed.

Thinking for a moment, Delano asked, "Has the paint analysis come back?"

"Not yet. Should be back soon. I'm betting they match. When the car was brought in, Kensie had it placed behind the truck. You'd have to be a blind man not to see the damage fits like a jigsaw puzzle."

"So when you going to charge her? Have you interviewed her?"

"She won't talk to me. Lawyered up as soon as she answered her door. I'm gonna wait till the paint analysis comes back." Taking a sip of his coffee, he looked at Delano. "You going to charge her for the murder of Clark?"

"No evidence. I got nothing…'cept a dead body…and a boat load of missing money from a fifty year old bank robbery."

"So remind me how they're connected?" Jackson had always been fascinated with cold cases.

"Like I said earlier, Becky, Gary and a guy named Cliff, the one Becky rode to the funeral with, are all half-siblings and the kids of one of the suspected robbers. Then you got Susan and Dewey who are siblings and the kids of another suspect. The guy Alleghany County locked up for breaking into Susan's house is the kid of the third suspect."

Taking in the information, Jackson thought for a moment. "Interesting how they've all come together. Especially after that money disappeared from the safe deposit box."

"Isn't it? Interesting that after fifty years the money has become the focus of their lives." Sipping his coffee, Delano was thinking. "Wonder what set all this in motion? Had to be something." Appearing to be lost in thought. Jackson suggested they write out a timeline of occurrences. "That's a pretty good idea." Two hours later, the timeline lay before them. Studying the paper, neither could determine the single event that put the rest of these deadly events in motion. "Look, I need to get back to the office. Why don't you come with me? I'll copy this for you and we can both study it. Maybe something will come to us."

Agreeing, Jackson paid the bill and followed Delano into the Federal building. Accepting the copy of the timeline, Jackson started for the door. "I'll let you know when the paint analysis comes back and I get the warrant for Becky."

~85~

As the trial got underway for the fatal accident of Gary Fitzgerald, Becky sat at the defendant's table trying to ignore the gallery full of people she grew up with and worked around. She could hear the whispers picking up an occasional "she", "guilty", and "sad". Not wanting to see their faces or look into their eyes, she sat staring forward not really seeing the judge's bench or the clerk busy organizing the paperwork for the Honorable H. Trumbo Bumgardner, Chief Justice for the Alleghany County Circuit Court.

Remorse filled Becky's being from the moment she realized what she had done that fateful morning allowing greed and paranoia to turn her into someone she never thought she would be. *I should have never run into him. But, he should have never gone to see Cliff.*

Having grown up in the area, Bumgardner had left long enough to attend college and law school at Georgetown. He interned for a justice on the Supreme Court during his first year out of law school which put him on the fast track to become a judge, and then chief justice. Returning home, he had bought a farm in Low Moor and started raising sheep, alpacas and cattle for relaxation when he wasn't on the bench. Most days weren't easy for him. Almost daily he had someone he knew, or someone related to someone he knew, come before him. Sentencing them to jail was never easy. This case in particular would be especially hard. Trumbo had attended the same church as Becky and their fathers had been friends, joining the Army together. He thought of recusing himself, but the justice brought in from another county may be harsher on her than she deserved. No. He felt he could be fair and impartial. At least he hoped so.

Having never married, he was free to pursue his love of baseball, traveling to every major league park in the country to enjoy a game. There had been talk after he had returned to the area that he might be gay. Nothing could have been farther from the truth. The one girl who had stolen his heart refused to marry him and move back to, in her words, "that podunk town where there is nothing to do but get fat and have babies." Instead, she remained in Washington with the movers and shakers joining him whenever he traveled to a stadium to see a game. She too was an avid baseball fan and loved his company, but not enough to give up the fast pace of the District.

As Bumgardner rapped his gavel calling for order, the gallery grew silent and those who could find a seat did so. The remaining spectators stood along the walls holding their hats in the hands. Some wore their Sunday best, others were in their work overalls, just coming off the rail yard. A few of the Bull Pen crowd filled the back row, most notably Junior Buzzard and Pat Patterson. Having appointed themselves as reporters for the rest of the guys from the Bull Pen who couldn't make it to the trial, they had agreed to meet early the next morning to give them the low down.

Delano sat in the front row of the gallery behind the prosecution with Jackson and Fisher. The spectators found it odd for a West Virginia trooper to be involved in the case. The surprise Delano had waiting for Becky gave him a sense of gratification. Surely today she would be found guilty of the murder of her half-brother, Gary. This day had been a long time coming.

Sitting in the front row behind Becky was Susan and Dewey. Not to show support for her, but to be able to hear every word spoken. They both liked Gary and believed that no one should have been left to drown in a river. Both had planned to be present in court until the verdict was read.

Opening statements seemed to last longer than usual for a bench trial. Normally the attorney's antics were reserved for juries, but under the advice of her court appointed attorney, Becky had chosen a bench trial. Her attorney, who was a "come here" only three years out of law school, had convinced her that with the popularity of the deceased and the news coverage in the paper, as well as on TV, it would make it next to impossible to find thirteen people who had not already formed an opinion of guilt about her. After contemplating his reasoning, she agreed to the bench trial knowing the judge would be a former Sunday school classmate.

The prosecution began with Grover Burgandine from Millboro Springs testifying about the morning he was returning from working first shift on the rail yard. Traveling the same route he drove every morning, he noticed the guardrail across the Cow Pasture River had been freshly damaged and the brush flattened leading down the embankment. Stopping, he saw the red pick-up nose down in the river with water flowing around the cab. "Did you go down the embankment to check the cab." The prosecutor asked.

"Yes, Sir. I did." Grover nodded his head.

"And what did you find?"

"I saw Gary laying over with his head underwater." Grover hung his head. "I tried to break the window but couldn't so I went up on the bank and got a rock."

"What did you do then?" The prosecutor prompted.

"I busted the window and tried to open the door…but I couldn't so I crawled through the window. Cut my belly too…on the glass."

"Was Mr. Fitzgerald alive?"

The defense attorney objected stating that Mr. Burgandine was not a doctor and couldn't say if he was dead or not.

The prosecutor pointed out that any human could tell if someone was breathing or not…it did not take a doctor or medical expert to determine if someone is breathing.

"I'll allow it." ruled the judge. "You can answer."

"He won't." Burgandine shook his head. "He was dead."

"Then what did you do?"

"I called the cops!" Burgandine declared matter of factly as the gallery laughed causing the judge to rap his gavel calling for order. The sudden sound of the rap caused Burgandine to jump in his seat.

"Thank you Mr. Burgandine." The prosecutor had no further questions for the witness.

The defense attorney stood stating he had no questions. Becky looked at him like he had lost his mind. Grabbing his arm when he sat down she whispered loudly, "Why aren't you going to ask him any questions?"

"Because we all know Gary was found in the truck dead. No reason to beat a dead horse."

The prosecutor then called Trooper Jackson. Questioning him about responding to the scene of the accident, Trooper Jackson confirmed what Mr. Burgandine had testified to. He went on to explain his process of photographing the scene and recovering dark blue paint transfer from the left rear fender and bumper of the truck. He then testified to attending the funeral of the victim and observing the last vehicle left in the lot. "Because of previous information I had learned about someone at the funeral, I ran the vehicle license plate and learned it was a rental from an auto body shop in Lewisburg, West Virginia. Responding to the body shop I was taken into the shop by the owner and directed to the vehicle of the person who had rented the vehicle left in the lot of the funeral home."

"And who was the person that had rented the car left at the funeral home and owned the vehicle found at the body shop?

Looking toward Becky, Trooper Jackson responded, "That would be Becky Fitzgerald."

"Was there any damage to Ms. Fitzgerald's vehicle?"

"Yes, Sir, there was."

Showing the trooper several photos of a dark blue vehicle with damage to the front right fender and bumper, he asked Trooper Jackson to describe what he was looking at.

"These are photos I took of the vehicle that belonged to Ms. Fitzgerald showing damage to her right front fender and bumper. This photo shows some red paint transfer that appears to be that of Mr. Fitzgerald's truck."

"Can you tell the court what you did after you photographed Ms. Fitzgerald's vehicle?"

Nodding toward Trooper Fisher, Trooper Jackson stated he contacted the West Virginia State Police and requested a unit respond to assist him. "I then accompanied Trooper Fisher to the magistrate where we, uhm, Trooper Fisher obtained a search warrant for the vehicle owned by Ms. Fitzgerald. We then returned to the body shop where the search warrant was executed by Trooper Fisher. The vehicle was seized and transported to the FBI forensics lab in Roanoke."

"And how did you maintain chain of custody of the vehicle for the two hour drive to Roanoke?"

"I followed the flatbed wrecker the entire way never losing sight of the said vehicle. It was then dropped at the forensics garage where the Forensics Tech took possession and secured it in her garage."

"And who was that Forensics Tech?"

"That would be Forensics Tech Kensie Blanc."

Handing Trooper Jackson an official looking document with the Virginia Department of Forensic Science embossed at the top, the prosecutor asked, "Could you tell us what this report is?"

Looking at the report, Trooper Jackson confirmed it was the lab analysis of the paint samples taken from Becky Fitzgerald's car and Gary Fitzgerald's truck.

"Can you read for the court what the report says?"

"Yes, sir. It, uh, states that the dark blue paint scrapings removed from the left rear fender and bumper of the truck driven by Gary Fitzgerald that was found in the Cow Pasture River match the dark blue paint scrapings of the vehicle that belongs to Becky Fitzgerald, the defendant."

"Now Trooper Jackson, looking at this second form, can you tell the court what this report says?"

Taking the second form, Trooper Jackson testified that the red scrapings removed from the front right fender and bumper of Becky Fitzgerald's vehicle matched the red paint of Gary Fitzgerald's truck.

"So, are you saying that the paint transfers from the two subject vehicles match?"

"Yes Sir."

"Thank you."

The defense attorney stood long enough to state he had no questions. Becky could not believe this guy. "Why are you not defending me?"

Looking at her, he once again told her there was nothing to ask. Everything was done per standard procedures.

Trooper Fisher was called to the stand next and confirmed everything Trooper Jackson had testified to about the search warrant. He also testified that the warrant had been filed with the circuit court in Lewisburg as well as the circuit court in Alleghany County, Virginia.

The prosecutor handed a copy of the search warrant to Trooper Fisher asking if that was the search warrant executed on Ms. Fitzgerald's vehicle. Trooper Fisher replied in the affirmative. "Thank you."

As with every other witness, the defense attorney had no questions. Becky came to the realization that she was going to be found guilty of aggravated vehicular manslaughter because she had no one fighting for her. She had never had anyone fighting for her. Being alone, even when she was living with her family, she always fought her own battles. Now, the biggest battle of her life and she wasn't being allowed to fight for herself. She had to depend on this incompetent boob who wouldn't ask a question if his life depended on it. *If I had that damn money I could afford to hire a real attorney, but nooooo, I'm stuck with this moron.* Becky came back to reality just as Kensie took the stand.

Identifying herself as the forensics tech for the Federal Bureau of Investigation, she confirmed she had found latent prints in the dark blue vehicle owned by Becky Fitzgerald. She stated that, although they were smeared prints, she was able to recover clear prints from the steering wheel as well as the inside and outside door handles belonging to Becky Fitzgerald and William Luther Clark. She also testified that she was able to compare the damage to Becky's vehicle with the damage to Gary's truck and found they fit like a jigsaw puzzle…perfectly.

Thanking Kensie for her testimony, the prosecutor then called the medical examiner who testified that Gary's cause of death was drowning as a result of being knocked unconscious when his head bounced off of the rear window of the truck. The medical examiner testified that the impact of the airbag deploying is what caused Gary's head to strike the rear window with sufficient force to knock him out. Alice also testified that because of Gary's position after being knocked unconscious, he inhaled enough water in his lungs to drown.

"So, you are saying that Gary Fitzgerald drowned as a result of injuries sustained from the accident?"

"Yes, sir. I am."

"Thank you. No further questions." The prosecutor announced to the court that the prosecution rests.

Turning to the defense attorney, Judge Bumgardner asked if he was ready to proceed. To the shock of the prosecutor and the crowd in the gallery, the defense attorney stated he had no witnesses. Becky knew this to be true. She had no alibi for the morning of the crash and no one was willing to stand up on her behalf to tell the court what a good person she was.

Hesitating, Judge Bumgardner asked Becky to stand. Stating that the evidence presented before him was overwhelming to prove her guilt, he was left with no other choice but to find her guilty of aggravated vehicular manslaughter.

Losing the strength in her legs, Becky collapsed in her chair. Her defense attorney standing beside her appeared not to notice as he requested a pre-sentencing report. He also requested that she be allowed to remain free on bond until her sentencing date.

Agreeing with the need for a pre-sentencing report, Judge Bumgardner felt he needed an in-depth report of Becky's background to determine if there was true malice behind her actions or if it was a result of poor judgment. "Sentencing will be set for forty-five days from today. As far as remaining free on bond, it is clear that although Ms. Fitzgerald grew up in the community, she no longer has any ties to the area which could make her a flight risk. Therefore, I am ordering she be held in the local jail until sentencing."

Becky began to weep. She knew her life was over and she would never see freedom again. The murmurs in the gallery grew as they heard the guilty judgment and then watched Becky fall back in her chair. The bailiff approached her. Taking her arm, he helped her stand as the gallery began to empty.

Walking toward Becky, Delano showed his credentials to the bailiff and identified himself as an FBI agent. "Excuse me bailiff, I have a piece of paper for Ms. Fitzgerald."

Becky looked at him. "What do you want?"

Handing the paper to the bailiff, Delano explained the paper was a warrant for the arrest of Becky Fitzgerald for the murder of William Luther Clark.

Becky collapsed to the floor as her attorney took the paper from the bailiff's hand. Examining the paper, he confirmed what the FBI agent had stated. Looking down at Becky, it was clear medics were needed. "You might want to call rescue." He stated. Soon Becky was being transported from the courthouse to the hospital at Low Moor. The bailiff was with her since she was now in the custody of the sheriff.

~86~

One week later, Susan and Dewey were back in court, but this time as a victim of a break-in. Muncy was escorted in wearing an orange jumpsuit with his legs in shackles and his hands handcuffed in front. His defense attorney requested the handcuffs be removed. Judge Bumgardner agreed as he looked out at the gallery. Noting the lack of crowd the Becky Fitzgerald trial had drawn, he did notice that Susan and Dewey were once again present.

"Mr. Muncy. You are charged with two counts of breaking and entering into a residence and two counts of possession of burglary tools." Judge Bumgardner began. "How do you plead?"

Standing, John Paul Muncy, Jr. addressed the court, "No contest, Your Honor." This response surprised the judge, his defense attorney and Susan and Dewey.

"Your honor, may I have a word with my client?"

Rapping his gavel, Bumgardner recessed the court for thirty minutes.

"Have you lost your freaking mind?" Scott, the defense attorney, could barely contain himself as they were escorted into the empty jury room. Do you realize you could be convicted of four felonies and sentenced to up to four years or more and fined at least ten thousand dollars? PLUS you'll lose a great deal of your civil liberties?"

Muncy looked at his attorney, "I do."

"Then WHY are you pleading no contest?"

"Because you and I both know I was caught in the act and they've got enough to convict me."

His attorney pointed out that reasoning was true for only one break-in. "You need to change your plea and let them prove you did the first break-in." Muncy considered the points made by his attorney. Re-entering the court at the end of the recess he advised the judge he had reconsidered his plea and would like to change it to not guilty. Noting the change, the judge asked the prosecution if he was ready to proceed.

"We are, Your Honor."

"Call your first witness."

The prosecution had only three witnesses; Susan, Dewey and the deputy who had pursued them to the house and pulled Susan off of Muncy. He called Susan first.

After being sworn in, Susan described the first time her house had been broken into. Stating that she had no proof because nothing was damaged, she felt a presence in the house. That disclosure caused Muncy to rolls his eyes. Susan saw him do so.

She then disclosed the installation of her security system because of the feeling she had after the first break-in. Describing the alert she received while at the funeral of Gary

Fitzgerald, she stated "I left the cemetery immediately and drove to my house. When I got there I caught Mr. Muncy coming out of my house through the backdoor. I ran after him under my house which is up on pylons and jumped on him and held him down until the deputy apprehended him."

"Ms. Nicely, who did you see entering your home without your permission and then subsequently caught leaving your house?"

Susan looked directly at Paul Muncy and pointed, "Him."

"Thank you."

Approaching the witness stand, the defense attorney asked if anything was missing from Susan's home after either of the break-ins.

Concerned that there wasn't, Susan was hoping her response would not have a negative effect on the outcome of the trial. "No, there wasn't."

"Thank you. No further questions." The defense attorney returned to the table where Muncy sat.

The prosecution called Dewey who testified the same as Susan. Not describing the harrowing ride to the cabin, he did describe the deputy following close behind and then taking control of Muncy once Susan had tackled him. The defense attorney had no questions for Dewey, excusing him.

The deputy described following Susan to the cabin, however, he failed to state he was pursuing her because of her speed and reckless driving. He did confirm that Susan gave chase to Muncy and tackled him as he ran from the cabin. Confirming that Muncy had burglary tools, he identified the lock pick set presented as evidence by the prosecutor. Finishing his questions, he turned the witness over to the defense attorney who had no questions.

Resting his case, the prosecutor awaited the defense attorney's defense.

Rising, the defense attorney called Paul Muncy to the stand. Susan and Dewey looked at each other with surprise. As he entered the witness stand, the clerk approached and swore him under oath. Taking a seat, Paul awaited the questions his attorney had prepared him to answer. The plan was to bring up the stolen money and the supposition that Susan had the money in her house.

"State your name, Sir," his attorney began.

"John Paul Muncy, Jr."

"Mr. Muncy, were you in the house of Ms. Susan Nicely?"

"Yes, Sir, I was."

"Can you tell the court why you were in her house the day she tackled you?"

"She had money that belonged to me and I wanted to recover it."

"Please explain," his attorney directed.

Paul Muncy looked at his hands in his lap. Not proud of his father's actions, he knew they were wrong, but he also felt he was entitled to the fruits of his father's crimes. "Well, you see, back in the early nineteen sixties my Dad and two other men were suspects in a bank robbery in Clifton Forge."

Interrupting the testimony, Scott asked Muncy to explain how he believed that.

"Well, my Mom kept a journal and when we, my siblings and me, were cleaning out her house, I found it. I took it home and started reading it. That's when I found out why my Dad wasn't home much. See, he used to take off for days at a time and then come home and things were all good."

"Did your father work?

"Yeah, he worked in the shipyard, but he took a lot of time off. At least that's what I was told. When I think back, he laid out a lot. What I know about the yard, if you miss too many days, they'll either fire you or suspend you. I think he got suspended instead of getting fired 'cause he was one of the few guys in the yard that worked on the nuclear-powered subs."

Scott interrupted again. "So, where did your father go when he would leave?"

Muncy shook his head. "I don't know, but I think a lot of times he came up here and hung out with his buddies Mr. Nicely and Mr. Fitzgerald." That revelation surprised Susan and Dewey. "I think they got the idea to rob the bank and Mr. Nicely kept the money. My Dad came home and I think he was going back to get his share, but then Mr. Fitzgerald died in the car crash and, I think, Mr. Nicely hid the money keeping it for himself."

The gallery gasped and then murmured to each other with this revelation causing the judge to rap his gavel bringing silence to the courtroom.

"Continue Mr. Muncy," Scott directed.

"So, I think Susan Nicely has the money in her house and I want my Dad's share."

"What makes you think Ms. Nicely has the money?" His attorney asked.

Muncy shifted in his seat. Looking at Susan sitting in the gallery, he continued. "Talk around town is the manager of the bank took some money out of her safe deposit box and the FBI found the money at his house. People were saying the FBI was saying it was part of the money taken in the bank robbery."

Scott interrupted. "So, how does Ms. Nicely fit into this."

"Well, the rumors around town are the money came from Susan Nicely's safe deposit box." The gallery gasped again and the judge, again, rapped his gavel. "I heard her box was empty so, I figured she had the money at the house and I was gonna get my Daddy's share." The gallery laughed and Paul became embarrassed. Mr. Scott encouraged him to continue. "So, I went to the house when she wasn't home. I just wanted the money."

"No further questions." Scott announced.

Eventually, the prosecutor stood. Approaching the witness stand he struggled to maintain his professionalism.

Not believing what he had just heard, he wasn't sure if Muncy seriously believed he was entitled to the stolen money. "So, let me clarify your testimony if you don't mind. Are you testifying that you broke into Susan Nicely's home to recover money that you believed was stolen by your father as well as Susan's father and another man during a bank robbery?"

Muncy didn't answer. Once he heard the prosecutor's summation of his testimony, he realized that his testimony was absurd.

The judge ordered Muncy to respond.

Turning toward the judge, Muncy stated that he would like to invoke his Fifth Amendment rights. The judge nodded as the prosecution stated he had no further questions.

Once the defense rested, the judge ordered a recess to consider the evidence presented to him. As he left the courtroom, Susan and Dewey knew Muncy would be convicted of at least one charge of breaking into her house and most likely the possession of burglary tools. Now they waited.

Thrilled when Muncy was sentenced to twelve months in jail and fined twenty-five hundred dollars, Susan knew he would not be a bother for at least a year, but she knew he would be back once he got out of jail. Somehow she needed to convince him that she did not have the money and had no idea where it was. That, she concluded, would be difficult.

~87~

As Susan entered the courthouse, she felt her entire life had been involved with the law since she moved back to Clifton Forge. Granted she was an attorney, but she was never on the receiving end of litigation. She was actually tiring of all the drama. *I moved back here to get away from drama and it seems to have followed me.* Choosing to sit in the back of the courtroom, she watched as Becky was brought in from the holding cell. Delivering a change of clothes to the jail before court, Susan felt Becky deserved a bit of dignity by not appearing in jailhouse orange. Requesting that it not be disclosed who her benefactor was, she felt no one should have to appear before a judge in a bright orange jumpsuit. She believed it would give Becky an unfair disadvantage and scream guilt. She also believed Becky would never accept the clothing if she knew who had provided it. The navy blue suit and cream colored blouse fit her perfectly which surprised Susan since she had to guess at the size. Guessing at her shoe size the navy pumps looked good as well.

Today was the day Becky would be tried for the murder of William Luther Clark. Having previously been convicted of the vehicular homicide of Gary Fitzgerald, she was still awaiting sentencing for that crime.

The courtroom filled with pretty much the same crowd who had appeared during her trial for the murder of Gary. Talk around town was that she was evil and needed to either serve time for the rest of her life for Gary's death, or at least receive a significant sentence for her crime. But, now with the trial of the death of Billy Clark, her life was on the line again and the citizens wanted her head.

Billy, like Gary, was a well liked guy. Billy however was left to move through life alone with a bone disease that could have, and eventually did take his life. He moved slowly when walking because of his bowed legs and never got involved in physical sports. Pool, bowling and darts were more his speed because he was less likely to break anything. His actions were considered odd by those who knew him and some thought him rude when they spoke into his left ear because he wouldn't answer them. The truth was, he couldn't hear them. He was deaf in his left ear…a result of his disease.

As the courtroom filled, Susan and Dewey took their seats on the back row which would allow them to slip out quietly. Susan had been subpoenaed to testify about the missing money from her safe deposit box, but the prosecutor caught her in the hallway outside the courtroom. "We may not need your testimony." Susan felt the relief wash over her. She truly didn't want to testify about the money. In fact, she didn't want to speak of the money at all in public. True, she had not stolen it. True, no one knew where the balance of the money was. True, her father, nor anyone else, had been convicted, let alone arrested, for the robbery. With Delano in the courtroom, she preferred to not have to testify at all.

As the judge entered the courtroom through the walnut backdoor that led to the judges' chambers, the bailiff commanded, "All rise! The Circuit Court for Alleghany County, the Honorable H. Trumbo Bumgardner presiding is now in session." The judge took his seat as well as everyone in the courtroom. Once the attorneys were greeted by the judge, he turned his attention to Becky.

"Good morning Ms. Fitzgerald. I see you are before me again for another charge of murder?"

Standing at the urging of her attorney taking her elbow and practically lifting her to her feet, Becky acknowledged his observation.

"Are you happy with this attorney?"

Nodding her head, she said she was. "I believe he will be much better than the last."

"And you choose to be tried by the court and not a jury?" Judge Bumgardner confirmed.

"Yes, your Honor. I do."

"Ms. Fitzgerald, you are charged with the murder of William Luther Clark. How do you plead?"

Looking directly at the judge, Becky responded, "Not guilty." She then bowed her head and stared at her finger tips supporting herself on the defense table.

"Be seated." The judge directed. "Mr. Prosecutor, call your first witness."

"The prosecution calls Junior Buzzard." Everyone in the gallery turned to look at Junior who they all thought was present just out of curiosity. Susan was as shocked as the rest of the crowd. *No wonder he is wearing his Sunday best.* All eyes were on Junior as he moved forward entering the well of the courtroom and standing before the witness box. Turning to face the bailiff as he approached with a Bible in his hand, Junior was directed to place his left hand on the Bible and raise his right hand. Junior did as directed.

"Do you swear to tell the truth and nothing but the truth so help you God?" The Bailiff asked.

"I do." Junior responded and then took his seat in the witness box.

After having Junior state his name and how he knew the defendant, the prosecutor asked if he knew the deceased, William Luther Clark. Junior nodded. The prosecutor reminded Junior he would have to answer all questions verbally.

"Yes, sir." Junior responded. "I knew Billy."

"How well did you know Billy?"

Junior explained they had gone to school together, attended church together and were both members of the Elks where they would see each other weekly and play darts together. "He also gave me a couple of loans at the bank."

"Can you recall ever seeing Ms. Fitzgerald and Mr. Clark together other than at the bank?"

"Yes, sir."

Junior was not known to be a talker in front of crowds or around strangers, so the prosecutor was having to draw his testimony out of him. Doing so, the defense would object stating he was leading the witness. Eventually, Junior testified that he was going fishing a few months ago out at Douthat and saw Becky and Billy at one of the picnic areas. Describing that it appeared they were in the midst of a heated argument.

"And why do you say that?"

"Well, Becky was right up in Billy's face and her arms were moving all about and then her finger was in his face and she grabbed his tie and pushed him backwards."

"Did you stop to see if you could help?"

Junior shook his head. "Oh no, sir." The members of the gallery laughed and the judge rapped his gavel calling order in the court. "You didn't get in between Becky when she was mad at anybody." Junior continued to shake his head. "No sir. Becky won't nobody you wanted to get on her bad side. She'd get you." The gallery laughed again and many who knew Becky nodded in agreement.

Again, the judge rapped his gavel. "I will clear the court if this continues." He announced.

"And how would she get you?" The prosecutor asked.

Junior shook his head, "Anyway she could. She's always been a scrapper. Just don't make her mad."

Once the prosecution completed their questioning, the defense took their shot at Junior. "So, Mr. Buzzard, you're riding down Douthat Road going fishing and you see all that?"

"Yes, sir." Junior nodded his head. "I drive slow cause the deer run across the road and I ain't wrecking my truck again." Members of the gallery nodded their heads confirming Junior's testimony again.

"So other than that one argument, have you ever seen Ms. Fitzgerald and Mr. Clark argue before or after?

"She argues with everybody." Not answering the question, Junior described how Becky was a hot head and would fight at the drop of a hat.

The defense realized if he continued to question this witness, he was digging his client's grave. "No further questions, your honor."

Next the prosecution called Cliff Burke. Cliff had not been in the courtroom during Junior's testimony. Nor was he seen in the hallway before court began. As the large walnut door opened, Cliff walked down the aisle making his way to the well and stood in the same place Junior had stood. Taking the oath to tell the truth he took the stand looking only at the prosecution. Doing everything he could to not look at Becky. When he wasn't looking at the prosecutor, he would look at his hands in his lap or the clock that hung above the doorway on the wall to his right that led to the jury room.

By the time he finished his testimony, he had explained how he had visited Billy one night late and Gary was there.

He stated Gary was acting a little squirrelly and had said his truck had broken down just down the road. Cliff continued to testify that he felt like there was more to Gary's visit than a broken down truck. "I offered to give Gary a ride home and he accepted. Then a few weeks later, actually, the night before Gary drowned in the accident, he came to my house and was telling me about the money and how Becky was all obsessed with it. He told me she made him go to Billy's house to get the money from him and for me to watch out for Becky. He said she would do whatever it took to get what she wanted."

"Objection! Hear say!" the defense stood.

"Sustained." The judge agreed. "Continue Mr. Burke."

"Anyway, that was after Becky and Gary were questioning me about how I built Susan Nicely's house and if I had installed a safe." That revelation shocked Susan and Dewey. Cliff continued. "Becky was real concerned about a safe and if I knew if there was any money in it."

"Mr. Fitzgerald, where did all this take place?"

"Well, Gary was at Billy's house out on Potts Creek. And then Becky and Gary talked to me at the tavern about the safe and all. Then Gary came to my house."

"No further questions." The prosecutor returned to his seat.

The defense began. "Were you afraid of my client?"

"Hell yeah I was afraid of her." The gallery laughed and the judge rapped his gavel. "Everybody is afraid of her.

She'll get you. We all know that. She's been like that since she was a kid."

The defense tried his best to repair the reputation of his client after asking the question, in hind sight he should have never asked. He needed to prove she was not a mean person. He could not tell if he was being successful with convincing the judge of that or not. He then stated he had no further questions.

Delano was called next. His testimony began with the missing money from the safe deposit boxes and then the investigation into the unsolved bank robbery fifty years earlier. Walking the judge through the investigation, he revealed that the money found buried at Mr. Clark's house was the same money taken in the robbery all those many years before. He revealed that three local men had been suspects in the robbery, but no arrests were ever made and the robbery had gone unsolved. One of those men was the biological father of the defendant as well as Gary Fitzgerald and Cliff Burke.

That revelation rocked the gallery. Murmurs became so loud the judge once again called for order and stated that the next outburst would cause him to clear the courtroom. Once the prosecution finished his questions, the defense had none to ask.

The next witness to be called was Alice. After testifying to the science of touch DNA and familial DNA she introduced the gloves that had been found in Gary's truck.

She testified that a small piece of brown canvas that was missing from one of Gary's gloves was found between the teeth of William Luther Clark during autopsy.

The gallery was so fascinated by this new science you could hear a pin drop; that and the fact that any further outbursts would have everyone thrown out of the court. And they ALL wanted to stay till the end.

Alice also testified that the cause of death was a result of a strong punch to Mr. Clark's face that broke his cheek bone and eye socket, and knocked him back onto a rock where he sustained sufficient injury to his head, causing sufficient blood loss for him to die.

"So, you are saying that Mr. Clark died as a result of a bump on the back of his head?" The prosecution sought to clarify her testimony.

"No, sir. What I'm saying is that Mr. Clark's death was a combination of the blow to the front of his skull, strong enough to break his cheek bone and eye socket, and the subsequent striking of his head on the rock that cracked open the back of his skull." The gallery gasped.

"So, it would have to be a really strong person to do such a thing, wouldn't you say?"

"No sir." Alice answered.

"And why is that? I mean, it takes a great deal or force to break a cheek bone and eye socket." The prosecutor smiled to himself. He knew the answer that was coming.

"Because Mr. Clark suffered from a disease called Osteogenesis Imperfecta."

"And can you explain to the court exactly what is Osteogenesis Imperfecta?"

Alice straightened in her chair. "Osteogenesis Imperfecta is commonly called Brittle Bones Disease. There are eleven varieties. Mr. Clark suffered from type four which is similar to type one which is the most common. It appears, from my examination that Mr. Clark at one time suffered from Scoliosis, which is a curvature of the spine and he had brittle teeth. Because of this disease, which is treatable, but not curable, Mr. Clark suffered many broken bones over his lifetime. His bones were so weak that anyone could have hit his face with enough force to break his cheek bone and eye socket. I would be willing to say that he never played any sports, nor did he play outside much because of the fear of breaking a bone."

Nodding his head, the prosecutor asked, "So, looking at the defendant, could you say that she was strong enough to break Mr. Clark's cheek bone and eye socket causing him to crack his head on the rock splitting his skull open?"

The defense attorney was out of his seat like a shot. "Objection! Calls for speculation!"

"I'll allow it." Judge Bumgardner responded. "I believe her medical expertise gives her the knowledge to respond."

Alice shifted in her seat again, "As I stated. Anyone could have struck Mr. Clark hard enough to break the bones."

"Thank you. No further questions."

The defense did his best to poke holes in Alice's testimony without success. He then returned to his chair beside Becky who never looked at him. She stared straight ahead.

Kensie was the final witness called for the prosecution. Her testimony was the bombshell that sealed Becky's fate. In her testimony she reviewed touch and familial DNA. She then testified that the money found at Clark's home had touch DNA that matched the DNA found on Mr. Clark's deceased body at the crime scene which matched Ms. Fitzgerald's DNA. Kensie then testified that when she examined the brown canvas gloves found in Gary Fitzgerald's truck, she cut them open and found a broken fingernail in the bottom of the ring finger of the right glove. Running DNA on the fingernail, she found that it too matched the DNA to Becky Fitzgerald.

Becky went from staring straight ahead to hanging her head low looking at her hands in her lap as Kensie testified. She knew she would be found guilty of Billy's murder as well. *Well Daddy, looks like neither of us are getting the money.*

Once again, the defense tried to poke holes in the testimony of this damaging witness without success. Once the prosecution rested, the defense brought forward character witnesses, but just as in the death of Gary Fitzgerald, Becky had no alibi and no one who could save her from her own actions. As the defense rested, the judge ordered a recess for lunch and advised the attorneys that closing arguments would begin upon their return at two o'clock.

The gallery was abuzz with speculation and conjecture. Susan and Dewey left as quickly as they could move through the crowd. Looking for Cliff, they wanted to have lunch with him, but he was gone…like a ghost.

~88~

Just before two o'clock, the gallery was once again filled. The prosecutor was at his table and Becky sat at the defense table refusing to look at anyone.

"All rise." The bailiff announced as he entered through the back walnut door just before the judge. "The Circuit Court for Alleghany County is back in session. Be seated."

"Mr. Prosecutor, are you ready for your closing arguments?" Asked Bumgardner.

The prosecutor stood and summarized for fifteen minutes the testimony of everyone who had come before the court before lunch. Pointing out the greed of the defendant and her attempt to manipulate other's to gain money that wasn't hers to begin with. When that failed, she took matters into her own hands killing the one person who had the money she believed to be hers and killing the other person who failed to recover the money. Reminding the court, Ms. Fitzgerald had already been found guilty of the murder of Gary Fitzgerald. The prosecutor then asked the court to find Ms. Fitzgerald guilty of the murder of William Luther Clark.

Once the prosecutor concluded his comments, the defense did his best to explain away Ms. Fitzgerald's actions and her past reputation for being one who always got what she wanted no matter what it took. After ten minutes, he asked the court to find his client not guilty.

Within a few minutes, Judge Bumgardner asked Becky to stand. He then asked if she had anything to say to the court before he pronounced sentence. She shook her head no. "Ms. Fitzgerald, I find you guilty of the first degree murder of William Luther Clark."

"Your honor. I ask that my client remain free on bail until sentencing."

The prosecutor immediately interjected, "Your honor. This defendant is awaiting sentencing for vehicular homicide. She was denied bond for that because she no longer has ties to the community. I ask that she not be allowed bond on this conviction as well."

Agreeing with the prosecution, Judge Bumgardner ordered Becky to be held in the county jail until sentencing. Just as with the previous conviction, he requested a pre-sentencing report. "This court is now adjourned."

Becky was led through the backdoor and returned to the jail. She was placed on suicide watch per the request of her attorney.

~89~

Returning to the courtroom two months after being found guilty of vehicular homicide of Gary Fitzgerald, her half-brother, and then first degree murder of Billy Clark, Becky once again stood before the Honorable H. Trumbo Bumgardner. The gallery was as full as it had been during both of her trials. Susan and Dewey sat in the back row; Susan grateful she never had to testify against her. She had once again delivered a suit to the jail for Becky to wear. This one a dark gray pin stripe with a soft pink blouse. The shoes delivered were black with a two inch heel. As before, the sheriff was asked not disclose who Becky's benefactor was. "She looks good, doesn't she?" Susan whispered to Dewey.

Dewey nodded. "Why are you so concerned about her looking good?" he whispered. "She killed two people."

Shrugging her shoulders, "I don't know," Susan hesitated. "Everyone deserves respect…and to look good when their life is coming crashing down around them." Dewey shook his head. "Besides, I hope someone would do the same for me if I was ever in that situation." The bailiff walked over motioning for them to be quiet.

As the judge listened to Becky's background, he took his glasses from his face and chewed on the ear piece. Seeming to doze, he closed his eyes. When the report was finished, he opened his eyes and asked Becky if what he had just heard was correct. Becky nodded. "Ms. Fitzgerald, as I have heard the evidence in both cases and I've had the opportunity to think about your cases; I find your actions egregious. I believe that your greed propelled you into actions that you believed were justified. Sadly, they were not. I'm not sure if you have learned anything from this." He waited.

Becky did not speak.

"In the case of Commonwealth v Fitzgerald concerning the vehicular homicide of Gary Fitzgerald, you were found guilty. I sentence you to fifteen years in prison and a fine of twenty-five hundred dollars. The reason for the additional five years is due to the gross, wanton and culpable actions that show a reckless disregard for human life. In the case of Commonwealth v Fitzgerald concerning the first degree murder of William Luther Clark, you were found guilty and I sentence you to thirty years in prison and a fine of fifty-thousand dollars. Ten years are to be suspended, however, you are to serve those ten years on probation once you are released from serving your sentence." Becky's head fell. "Your sentences are to run concurrently." With nothing more, the judge rapped his gavel adjourning the court.

As the bailiff moved toward Becky, Susan sat in the back row. She knew Becky deserved to serve time for what she had done, but she was looking at twenty years of her life behind bars. In Virginia there is no possibility of parole thanks to Governor George Allen who had abolished it in nineteen ninety-eight. *So sad.* Susan thought. *So many lives destroyed over something our fathers put in motion so many years ago.* Dewey took Susan's arm helping her to stand. "Let's go. Let's find Cliff."

Driving into Clifton Forge, Susan suggested they stop at the tavern for a beverage. "I need it." Dewey parked on Ridgeway Street just down from the tavern. Walking in, they found Cliff at her favorite table drinking a beer. "Mind if we join you?" Susan asked. Cliff waved his hand toward the chairs.

"How much time did she get?" Cliff had not been in court. He knew she would be sentenced to a long time in prison and he believed his testimony had contributed to it.

"She's serving twenty years total and then ten years probation." Dewey responded. "It'll be a long time before she sees the outside." Susan couldn't speak. She just sipped on her Jack Daniels and listened to Cliff and Dewey talk about the trial.

~90~

It had been a whirlwind of a year since Susan had chosen to return to Clifton Forge. Now, as the weather was warming, she greeted her three siblings who had never bothered to visit. *Why should they?* They had their lives and she was keeping them informed about the progress of the house. But, today was the grand unveiling.

Hugs all around followed by drinks. Dewey eventually fired up the grill and Susan prepared the steaks for cooking. Janice made the salads while Jack and Bill just sipped on their beers. Stories were told and everyone got the grand tour. As the sun set behind the mountain the night sounds began. Tree frogs called out and an occasional rustle of bushes peaked everyone's interest. Eventually moving inside, they listened to music and cleaned up the mess from the meal.

"I have something for ya'll," Susan announced once everyone had consumed several drinks and were very much relaxed. Leaving the great room, she returned carrying three boxes wrapped in Christmas paper and hug bows.

"It's not Christmas!" Janice exclaimed.

Susan grinned. "I know, but once you open these boxes you'll think it is." She laughed.

Tearing into the wrapping, the siblings were super excited to see what the boxes contained. "WAIT!" Susan called. "I want ya'll to open them at the same time." Dewey grinned. He already knew what she was doing. He had received his gift before the siblings arrived. With all the paper in the floor, Susan announced. "When I count to three, pull the top off of your box. Ready? One. Two. Three!"

As the tops came off, the mouths flew open, "Money?" Jack appeared confused along with Bill and Janice.

"Yep. Money," Susan confirmed. "Twenty-eight thousand dollars!" She couldn't help but grin.
The looks on her sibling's faces was priceless.

"Where did you get all this money?" Bill asked. "Did you rob a bank?" Susan and Dewey burst out laughing.

"You could say that." Dewey confirmed. With that, Dewey and Susan began the saga of the stolen money starting all the way back with the initial robbery and taking them through all of the events of the past year. Most of the time the siblings sat with the mouths hanging open. Occasionally asking questions, they continued to drink; the girls wine, the guys beer.

The hands of the clock moved into the early morning hours. By the time all questions were answered and the entire story had been told, everyone was thoroughly toasted and exhausted.

Dewey stood. "Well, I believe it's time for bed. Susan has a place to secure your presents until you leave."

"Yes, I do. And, I would strongly recommend that you never deposit the money in any bank. As we told you about them finding the money at Billy's, they were able to trace the money back to the robbery." Susan stood directing her siblings to bring their money. "They can't get us for robbing the bank since I'm thinking we were all a little too young to drive," they all laughed. "But, the insurance could file a claim and the Feds could file an asset forfeiture claim."

"Well, I think the bank got its money back through the FDIC." Jack pointed out.

Dewey reminded him that the bank is out of business. They all laughed. "And screw the Feds. They confiscate enough assets from drug dealers. They don't need this." They all laughed again.

ALSO BY STEWART GOODWIN

An Imperfect Oath
Hunter Hunted
The Guardian
Lessons Learned; A Practical Guide For Care Givers
Letters From Home; 1946-1947
The Twisted Tree; Genealogy of Rockbridge & Augusta Counties
I, The People

ORDERING INFORMATION
Copies of all of Stewart's books can be ordered at

www.StewartGoodwin.net
www.squareup.com/store/stewart-goodwin
Amazon.com

Like Stewart on Facebook at
https://www.facebook.com/StewartGoodwin20/

ABOUT THE AUTHOR

Born in Clifton Forge and growing up on the Virginia Peninsula, Stewart's adult years were spent in public service; first in law enforcement assigned to patrol, narcotics and community policing and then as an educator. Stewart has traveled throughout Europe, the Americas and the Caribbean. Those experiences and events are the basis of her books.

Her first book, "An Imperfect Oath" is loosely based on a true crime in which she was to dine with the suspect the night of the murder.

Stewart currently lives on her farm in Central Virginia.

Made in the USA
Middletown, DE
05 February 2025